Acclaim for Keir Weimer's

A QUEST FOR REDEMPTION

Stories from Prison

"Keir Weimer's prison stories are not your typical prison stories. Keir Weimer is not your typical prisoner. White, educated, privileged, athletic, he spends almost four years behind bars for vehicular manslaughter. In that time he confronts the terrible tragedy of his and his addiction's making. He lays before us the precariously strange, violent, often hopeless world behind the razor wire: the terrible fraternity of gang bangers, conmen, addicts and their keepers who create a parallel universe of laws, politics, economics, healing, and, yes, even a subset of heroes and villains. *A Quest for Redemption: Stories from Prison* is smart, literate and compelling. A book you must read."

-Mary Sanders Shartle
Award-winning poet,
Author of *The Hermit: the Truth and
Legend of Lily Martindale*, SUNY Press

"With a sense of longing, I believe that Keir Weimer's book, *A Quest for Redemption: Stories from Prison*, springs from a place deep within. It is a place rooted in heartbreak, stemming from choices made on a carefree summer day, in the height of Keir's youth. Those choices culminated in a life tragically lost, and many other lives forever changed. Keir's stories from prison were indeed written while incarcerated; we learn what life in prison is like and we hear true accounts of despair and anguish surrounding life on the inside.

Poignantly, these stories mirror Keir's own journey of discovery, transformation and redemption, as he personally struggles to find more than freedom from his own broken past. There is a genuine sincerity and hopefulness that rings throughout each of these stories, and I believe they are cathartic for anyone who suffers a loss. Keir provides solace through these compelling stories by his ability to pull light out of the darkness."

-Marianne Smith Dalton
Fine Artist, Photographer, Curator
(www.mdaltonart.com)

"Keir Weimer speaks from the heart about his personal struggles and desire to make a positive impact in the lives of young people. *A Quest for Redemption: Stories from Prison* is an excellent book, but what I love most is that the proceeds will benefit those less fortunate. That makes the book a powerful example of his dedication to giving back to society."

-Matt Bellace, PhD
Speaker, Psychologist, Comedian

"Having spent most of my career in criminal justice, I hope Keir Weimer's experiences can clearly give the message that drinking and driving can be murder. While young folks consider themselves invincible doing what everyone else is doing, "just having fun," Keir's wake-up call was time in New York State prison. He will live with the consequences of his reckless behavior for the rest of his life. Hopefully, Keir's reflections will reach as many young people as possible to save lives, maybe even their siblings or best friends."

-Pat Tappan
Formerly...
Commissioner, NYS Division of Parole
Commissioner, NYS Commissioner of Corrections
Commissioner of Corrections,
Onondaga County, New York State

ABOUT THE AUTHOR

K eir Weimer resides in Saratoga Springs, NY. Keir is a grateful entrepreneur, serving as President and Founder of The Thistle Island Group, LLC, a real estate investment and holding firm he founded in January of 2012. He is also a licensed Realtor with Select Sotheby's International Realty, based in Saratoga Springs and serving clients both there and throughout the Adirondack Park. Keir has also come to embrace pursuits as both a writer and an active inspirational speaker, telling his story and carrying the message forward to students, prisoners and a variety of audiences. Keir enjoys reading, writing, traveling and exploring new areas and challenges in life. He's an accomplished triathlete, alpine and water skier, all-season hiker, sailor and all-around outdoor and Adirondack enthusiast. He can be reached at his personal website, found at www.keirweimer.com, or at his book's website, found at www.aquestforredemption.com.

A QUEST FOR REDEMPTION

*Stories
from Prison*

KEIR WEIMER

This is a work of creative nonfiction. The stories and experiences contained herein are all true. Some names and locations have been changed, to protect the privacy of the individuals and the security of the institutions in which these stories were written.

For Tiffany, forever...

CONTENTS

Stories

AUTHOR'S PREFACE

On November 23rd, 2007, I stood numb in front of a Supreme Court judge, as he sentenced me to serve 2-6 years in New York State prison for vehicular manslaughter. I was quickly ushered away by the attending deputies to my new life and reality behind bars. I was in shock...I was lost...I was broken. This was the end—but it was also the beginning.

I had been responsible for an alcohol-related boat accident in the Adirondack Park of New York State the previous summer; an accident that claimed the life of a beautiful young woman named Tiffany Heitkamp. I was fully responsible for this tragedy, and not a day goes by where I don't think about Tiffany, and the commitment I have made to her and her memory for the remainder of my life. This obligation I speak of is a duty I have come to embrace: I must advance the powerful message contained in this tragedy and my life's narrative forward.

I hit life's lowest bottom sitting alone in prison, as I confronted the weight of my guilt and the myriad of emotions that resulted from being responsible for the taking of another person's life. The accident was not just an accident, I came to realize, but rather the culmination of years of misplaced attitude and careless behavior on my part. It had been almost a year since I had been sent to prison for what I had done. Then one cold, introspective evening—after two of the darkest years of my life—the truth finally sank in: the accident had been preventable, and was due to my long history of alcohol abuse. I had hit my true bottom. When I finally came to terms and admitted to myself that I had a huge alcohol problem, the haze began to clear and I knew what I had to do.

I made a commitment that night...to Tiffany, to my family and to myself: I was going to live a sober life, and not let this horrible tragedy claim two lives. I was going to get brutally honest with myself, face my demons head-on, and recover as a person determined to bring something positive to this situation. I was going to repurpose my life for the betterment of others, by spreading the powerful message contained in this painful story to those that needed to hear it.

Every day since that lonely day in prison has been better and more positive than the previous. I decided early on in my prison term that I would not count time, but rather make time count. I seized this opportunity in every sense, so I could grow and mature, heal from all the pain I had caused and lived in, and get to a point where I was healthy enough to help others. With my old Smith Corona typewriter raring to go, I began to write. Writing was an outlet for me, a way I could escape the confines of my physical and emotional imprisonment, and find solace.

This book is a collection of narratives from prison. All of the events are true, and the stories are told as authentically as possible. Only the names of individuals and some of the locations have been changed, in the interest of privacy.

These stories delve individually into a varied exploration of the human condition and experience, and together they strive to build a larger narrative that unites a host of themes. The stories were written in the moment; as a form of catharsis for me, as a form of journalism for the public, and hopefully as a way to make others look at the world and their lives through maybe just a slightly different lens.

It is my sincere hope that these stories can incite reflection and inspiration in those that read them. I hope they prompt questions that might not have been considered before...about human nature, government, politics, ethics and more. I hope they might allow for a new and unique way in which an individual can relate to a world largely foreign and unknown, through the struggles and emotions that we as humans all share, and that transcend even the highest prison walls.

ACKNOWLEDGEMENTS

First and foremost, I'd like to thank my family, for their unwavering and continued support through an extremely difficult six years for many. My father, Mark Weimer, my mother, Gail Doering, and my younger brother, Jared Weimer, have given me nothing but unconditional love, and made me at times wonder if I was even worthy of such. I could not have gotten through the pain, the tragedy and the imprisonment were it not for them and their strength. I'd also like to acknowledge how invaluable my father was in the editing, collating and preparation of the manuscript. Thank you dad, mom and Jared for your unconditional love and support, I'm forever grateful.

There were also several great friends and people along the way that gave me the encouragement and support I needed to persevere and move forward positively. I'd like to thank Lee Jokl, an amazing friend and confidant for over fifteen years. Besides my immediate family, Lee was the only person to whom I regularly and clandestinely mailed each completed story, once the last period had been punctuated by my dusty type-writer. As my family members did, Lee provided valuable feedback and suggestions on how to improve the stories. For this and his continued support as a loyal friend, I'm grateful.

I'd like to thank Joy Gillis, for her amazing support and consistent correspondence from afar. I want to thank my cousin Erik Holmgren and his wife Beth for their support, as well as my uncle Craig Doering and his wife Carolina for theirs. I'd like to thank Martha Hanson for her support and correspondence. I'd also like to thank the following friends for their support and commitment to correspond while I was in prison: Briana Huffer, Jason Dambrauskas, Kelly Vergamini, Shannon Jones, Joe O'Brien, Jacqueline Bates, Alex Nitka, Imran Ansari, Charles Johnson, Chris Stoner, Susi Ricker and Claire Dwyer. For everyone else I'd like to name and thank, but cannot due to the constraints of brevity, thank you.

I'd like to thank the incomparable Mary Sanders Shartle, a writer and ambassador of all things artistic by profession, and a wonderful person by nature. Mary provided me with precious feedback and editorial advice, for which the project would not have been the same without. Her acumen and candor are much appreciated, and I'm grateful for her work and her friendship. I'd like to thank Marianne Smith Dalton for her support for this project, and for her help in collaboration. I'd like to thank Matthew Bellace, PhD, a very talented writer and motivational speaker, for his support of this book and my speaking efforts. I'd like to also thank my professional editor and proofreader, a sharp-witted Aussie from the Gold Coast that goes by the name of Jim.

I'd like to thank Clark Lubbs of Old Forge, NY, for his talented work on the author portrait. I'd like to thank Trisha Barnes, a very talented public relations and marketing professional, for her amazing work on the PR and marketing campaigns for the book. I'd also like to thank the talented Nicholas Wakeman, for his work on developing the message and framework for the website, and then translating that vision into a beautiful and functional home for the book, and related speaking and charitable activities.

To everyone else who has helped or assisted me along the journey that has been the past six years of my life, thank you. I am forever grateful for this, and so much more.

A NOTE ON THE BOOK'S PROCEEDS

Keir Weimer has decided to donate all of the proceeds from the sale of this book to charity. In an effort to more formally organize and bring both structure and accountability to his activities as an author and inspirational speaker, at the time of this book's printing, Keir Weimer is considering the incorporation of a nonprofit organization.

He believes this tax-exempt status will aid his efforts, so that all of the proceeds from the sale of this book, as well as any speaking fees generated by his speaking engagements, can be brought in tax-free, and then immediately paid out to the network of charitable organizations he's selected that share his same values and mission to educate, spread awareness, and inspire others.

If you'd like to learn more about this, the charitable organizations Keir Weimer intends to donate to, or anything else about where the proceeds from these efforts will land, please visit his personal website at www.keirweimer.com, or his book's website at www. aquestforredemption.com. Thank you for your interest in this book, and for your support of this effort and all that it seeks to accomplish.

STORIES

THE AMBUSH

It was mid afternoon, and Wayne had just returned from his afternoon program at the prison's educational wing. It was a sunny but cool day in western New York, warm enough though to have the windows in our room open halfway. Tom was the only other roommate in the room, besides me. He was deep in some obscure fantasy novel, with no regard for much else. Nothing new there. Wayne looked fatigued. He sat on his steel bed in the corner of the five-man room we all shared, our two other roommates still not back from their afternoon programs. We chatted for a minute, about nothing really. I had been busy when Wayne arrived, and made a point of being terse in our conversation. Wayne liked to talk. He liked to talk a lot. You might say he had "the gift of gab."

Wayne was about my age, in his late twenties. He was about six foot, probably two-thirty, maybe even two-forty. He was the classic endomorph: thick, doughy and slightly rotund. In spite of this, he was committed to bettering his physique. He frequented the weight-pit regularly, did some light calisthenics a few times a week, and generally gave the impression he was really making exercise and fitness a priority in his life. The problem, however, was tripartite in nature: absolutely no cardio exercise, downright horrible genetics, and six-thousand-plus calories a day.

When Wayne finally took my shortness as a hint, he took off his shoes and laid back on his bunk, the latest James Paterson novel in hand. The room became quiet, if ever so briefly. Suddenly, one of our neighbors from across the hall came into our room unannounced, with aggressiveness in his gait. He was wearing what appeared to be some sort of handball or weight-lifting gloves. He went directly to Wayne's bunk, and got in his face.

"Super-tough, huh? Super-tough? Nah…I'm not super-tough…this is me, motherfucker," he said as he lunged at Wayne.

He laid three hard punches into Wayne's unassuming face, Wayne and all of us in shock.

"This is me, motherfucker. Super-tough nothing, you faggot! This is me, you motherfucker!!!"

He unleashed another flurry of punches, just bashing Wayne's face as he lay face-up on his bed, completely defenseless to the onslaught.

"What the fuck, Slug? Let me get my fucking shoes on at least, man! What the fuck?" Wayne uttered in desperation, trying to buy a brief reprieve.

At this point Tom had stopped reading, which was rare. I was standing up, in total shock from what had just gone down. I didn't know what to do. I was horrified at what I had just seen happen to my friend and roommate. I was also instantly plagued with a deep sense of ambivalence and guilt. What should I do? Wayne was bleeding heavily from his right nostril, and his eye looked like it was beginning to swell up. He stood up hesitantly, reaching without purpose for his shoes. Right when he bent over to try and put them on, and take a stand, Slug came charging forward again. Two hard body blows to the torso this time. Wayne buckled slightly, hunching in pain from the impact.

"What the fuck!?! I don't even have my shoes on!" Wayne uttered in a pleading defense to stop.

He put up no defense though, despite now being at least on his feet.

"Fuck you, you piece of shit," Slug gibed condescendingly, lunging forward for another strike.

This time he threw his body's inertia into a devastating uppercut to Wayne's already-bloodied chin, knocking him back onto his steel bunk with certain finality.

Silence. Shock. I was stuck; Tom was stuck.

"If you want more, I'll be in the bathroom waiting. I'll give you your five minutes…if you want it," Slug said as he stood over Wayne.

He turned and left our room. Silence prevailed, again. Wayne was now covered in blood. His nose was bleeding, his chin was cut and swelling, and his eye was closing by the second. He was just as stunned as all of us.

As soon as Slug left, however, Wayne began to posture for face. He kept going back to the shoes.

"I didn't even have my shoes on! What the fuck... how cheap is that? How am I supposed to fight without my shoes on?" he kept saying rhetorically, expecting no reply from us.

Even if he solicited a reply, I don't know what I would have said. I couldn't believe what had just happened in a matter of minutes. Tom and I exchanged glances, each looking to the other for some kind of initiative or direction as to how to respond to this situation.

Nothing. Finally, after an inappropriate period of silence from us both, the only response I was able to muster was:

"What the heck was that all about?"

Wayne sat on his bunk, staring blankly into his apparently interminable locker. He didn't answer me. Shit, I wouldn't have answered me. I felt horrible. I had just watched a roommate and a friend get brutally beaten up not ten feet from my bed, and I stood like a spectator and did nothing.

I knew what Wayne was thinking; he expected me to intercede, to get his back. At bare minimum, try and break it up. Nope. Nothing. Stuck. I knew instinctively that nothing good would come out of the situation— even less than did in the end—should I have gotten involved. I would have either gotten my ass beat too, later gone to solitary confinement, just made a fool of myself, or possibly all of the above. I kept thinking of how I had an approaching Parole Board hearing, my first and best chance at release. I thought of my family, and what they would think if I jeopardized coming home for this...for something that didn't involve me. I began to feel a bit better. I was okay with my decision, even glad. This didn't lessen the guilt or empathy I felt for Wayne, however.

He was bleeding pretty badly into a sock he had grabbed as a cloth. He was still working on something in his locker. I decided I had to go over and attempt to console him. I approached him and offered some words of comfort, asked if he wanted me to get him some ice for his face. When I peered over his locker door, I saw what he had been fashioning. He had placed a Master lock into the bottom of one of his long state tube socks, and was tying it off at the base. I asked him suspiciously what he intended on doing with this makeshift prison mace.

"I gotta do what I gotta do," he replied sullenly.

Again I was shocked. I was shocked at his response to what had happened, shocked at this developing situation. I immediately counseled against any such action with this medieval-like bludgeon, but I was met by deaf ears. He was mad, embarrassed, humiliated in front of everyone, in a place where all you have is your pride and your word. I began pleading with him, knowing how regrettable any outcome would be, should that weapon leave our room.

All of a sudden, Slug returned, stopping at our door.

"You coming or what? It's been five minutes. You want some more or what?" he said in a jeering tone.

Wayne was stuck now; he didn't know what to do. I could tell. He had already been humiliated once. He couldn't bear to go through that again in front of everyone... especially now that his shoes were on.

He got up from his steel bunk, rather reluctantly. The weapon he made lay on his bed. The two started exchanging barbs before Wayne was even out of our room. Then fists went up, and the bathroom as venue was swiftly forgotten. They immediately spilled across the hall into another five-man room. There were only two people in this room at the time, one of whom was an old-timer named Jack, a friend of mine. He promptly sensed the danger, got up from reading the Wall Street Journal which I had just given him not an hour before, and made a swift beeline toward the recreation room. The other person in the room just stood up from his bunk and remained motionless. Tom and I didn't know what to do...again. We instinctively stood at our own doorway, watching this developing fight, and keeping an eye out for the correctional officers.

Slug delivered a few quick jabs to Wayne's jaw, another to his other eye. Blood flew across the room, splashing the neighboring bunk's white sheets, and leaving a clear record not too open for dispute. This certainly wasn't Slug's first fight. Then a forceful blow from Slug landed directly on the side of Wayne's nose, stunning him and sending him stumbling backward. Slug took the opportunity and rushed Wayne, driving him into the ground and straddling his chest. He proceeded to lay a torrent of haymakers directly into Wayne's undefended face. Blood splattered from each side of his face, in all directions. I cringed and was horrified at what I was powerless to stop. The sheer brutality and inhumanity of this act was overwhelming.

I wanted to jump in and pull this beast off Wayne, but I was fixed. I wanted to yell to Wayne to at least cover his face, and block some of the blows, but I couldn't. Slug didn't stop. He just kept laying into Wayne's almost motionless face with his bloody gloves. Finally, finally, Slug decided it was enough. He got off of Wayne's stomach, and turned to walk out of the room and proceed with his day. He had the look on his face of someone who'd just finished his job. He stopped for a moment, and stared menacingly at Tom and me, as if to signal we were next if we said anything. I pretended unsuccessfully that I hadn't been watching, and that it was nothing. My insouciance must have been clearly disingenuous. Slug knew it. Luckily for us, he kept walking.

When I turned my attention back to Wayne, I saw him stand up slowly and begin to head for our room. When he came into view at the doorway, I wasn't even sure it was him; he looked like a different person. His eyes were both swollen shut to mere slits in his face. His nose was swollen and bleeding profusely down his face and chin. There were lacerations above both eyes, on his chin and on his left cheek. He was almost unrecognizable. I immediately felt intense guilt and regret for not having done anything. Twice, now. I approached him and guided him back to our room by the arm. I helped lay him down face-up on his bed. We said nothing to each other. Tom stood like a statue in awe of Wayne's appearance.

I asked him if I could get him some ice. He nodded. I quickly left and went to the recreation room to get the ice. I was in a state of shock at the level and intensity of this violence, all over a petty comment made by Wayne in jest, a comment that was entirely devoid of malevolence. I tried to think of what I would say to Wayne upon my return. How could I console, provide comfort, explain my behavior? Nothing came to me as I entered the recreation room to retrieve the ice. But I remembered all too clearly what had sparked it.

* * *

Just hours earlier that day, Wayne had been pacing around the room awaiting the afternoon program movement call, which would be broadcast on the dorm's PA system. They were late calling it; it was already past twelve thirty. I was trying to read, but it wasn't working out. Wayne was bad at picking up subtle hints. Or maybe he was fully aware, and went ahead anyhow. Whatever the case, I found it a little disrespectful. I put the book down, a bit peeved, and entertained Wayne in conversation.

We began discussing past albums of the hip-hop artist Jay-Z, and when some of his early work was released. I used to listen to some of his music in high school and college, so I was able to engage him. This made Wayne laugh. He found it funny how a white kid from the suburbs could be so informed in this area. I could at least appreciate the irony in this observation.

Wayne quizzed me on the most popular single from *The Life and Times of Shawn Carter, Volume One* album, and when exactly it hit the airwaves. I gave him an answer he thought was incorrect. I insisted I was correct.

"That was one of my favorite Jay-Z songs. I think I'd know what album it was on and when it was released," I retorted.

He wouldn't budge though, and kept saying I was wrong.

"Why don't you just pull out the album from your locker, and we'll see right now who's right and who's wrong," I replied.

He stared at me with a quizzical fix.

"I do have that tape, don't I," he said, awestricken.

He quickly went to his locker, entered the combo and flung open the doors. He grabbed his shoebox where he kept his cassette tapes, and went rummaging for the album. He looked up at me blankly.

"Slug must still have it. Fuck."

He put the box back, and closed his locker. He went to the door of our room, and peered into the room across the hall where Slug slept.

"Yo, Slug, I need that Jay-Z tape back, I gotta prove a point to my roommate," Wayne said.

Slug stared at him without moving, and replied, "You can get it when you come back from your afternoon program. My locker's already locked and I'm about to leave," he said to Wayne.

Wayne looked a bit irked.

"Just get in now real quick, man; they haven't called movement yet and I wanna just prove a point now," Wayne said in reply.

"TWELVE-THIRTY PROGRAM MOVEMENT GOING OUT," the officer broadcast down the gallery on the dorm's PA system.

"See, it's time to go anyhow. Don't make me repeat myself, Wayne. When I told you I'd give it back after program, I meant I'd give it back AFTER program," Slug said roughly.

Wayne made his way out into the gallery, heading for the stairwell as Slug sat back on his bunk, lacing up his Timberlands.

"All right, Slug, you're super-tough now, huh? Whatever, man," Wayne said, as he left for afternoon program, visibly annoyed.

* * *

The recreation room was alive when I entered, more so than usual. As I walked over to the corner to get the ice, I saw Slug sitting in the opposite corner, surrounded by his platoon of followers. He was being exulted for his violent achievement; hailed for beating Wayne to a bloody pulp. This guy looked like Mayweather after a knockout, literally, as if what he did, and why he did it, was somehow laudable. I was disgusted. Infuriated. But I knew I could do nothing.

Before I even reached the ice, I was stopped by three guys; two old-timers who'd both been in prison over thirty years, and a younger guy probably closer in age to me. They knew I was Wayne's roommate and friend. They gave me a spiel on Wayne, and what I needed to tell him when I returned to our room. They told me how Wayne needs to keep his fucking mouth shut, and not snitch on Slug. They told me how he needed to be a man, and not tell the cops what happened and who beat him so badly.

I was outraged at the gall of these men, these men who hadn't witnessed the vile brutality of what had just happened to an innocent, good-hearted man. These men had lived in this topsy-turvy environment for so long they now thought this was the right thing to do. The moral compass had become completely flipped. I nodded and said sure, whatever, and left to go back to the room with the ice.

I sat on the edge of Wayne's bed and sealed the ice in an old mess hall bread bag. Then I wrapped it in a state hand towel, and handed it to Wayne. His face had gotten worse in just the few minutes I'd been gone. He could barely see, he muttered. His face was covered in dried blood blotches and canals. His open wounds appeared to be clotting at least. He was in bad shape.

He told me his head was throbbing like crazy, and he felt nauseous. I went to my locker and found a couple of two hundred milligram ibuprofens. He threw them back quickly and laid back down on the pillow, ice now covering most of his face.

Not even a half-hour had elapsed, when suddenly three officers came rushing into our room, and went straight to Wayne's bunk. They asked him to stand up and remove the bag of ice from his face. He very slowly complied. The three officers shuddered and winced, but didn't turn away out of an eerie fascination with the damage sustained by the beaten. It was a dispiritingly inhuman interest that seemed to go beyond their duty. It was almost amusing to them. They ordered Wayne to go with them, left the room and headed toward the officer's station at the end of the gallery.

After they had left, Tom and I and about thirty other inmates peering out of the rooms that lined the gallery, watched as Wayne was handcuffed and placed face-first against the ashen cinder block wall. Right next to him, Slug was already cuffed and flush with the wall, two officers behind him talking with a sergeant. Looking down the hall, you could see an air of unconcern, yet no one could stop watching the steady and reliable hand of administration at work. And then the two were departed, promptly taken away to solitary confinement.

The talk continued on the dorm unit about how Wayne must have been a snitch. How else could the authorities have known so quickly? Everyone was beginning to say this, even people who I thought were his friends. They said they'd known he was a snitch all along, how they had that feeling, and how this had proved their hunch was right. I thought to myself this was ridiculous! This was complete bullshit! I had to defend Wayne's honor; I had to defend the truth! Wayne had never left the room after the fight, so how could he have snitched? How could he have told the correctional officers if he never left his bunk?

It didn't matter though. The talk continued, and the rumors began to solidify. Wayne had been brutally beaten almost to unconsciousness, and now he was being victimized yet again. He was humiliated, embarrassed and demeaned. Now he was suffering another attack, only this attack would prove much more destructive. He was now being affixed with the label of a snitch—a reputation with the worst ramifications in prison. If thirty days in solitary confinement wasn't bad enough for having been the one severely beaten, this new and untrue reputation would prove to be much, much worse. I tried and I tried…but it was too late. It didn't matter now. Minds had been made up, and Wayne was the bad guy.

PRISON ECONOMICS

It doesn't matter where I am. I might be in the yard running, I might be working out, I might be on the walkway to a call-out, or simply on the way to chow... but one thing's certain: it never differs. I'll be bombarded with offers. There are always at least a couple, and sometimes as many as six. Everyone wants to buy my pseudo designer shades; they want my faux Dolce & Gabbana aviator throwbacks. The offers always start way above actual value, and then they climb. Oh, how they climb. An opportunist would have dealt with the ultraviolet inconvenience of the sun a long time ago, and behaved rationally. Neo-classical micro-economists would have smiled with smug delight at this play. But no, not me. I wouldn't budge, no matter how inflated the offers got.

I was in possession of a commodity that could no longer be procured on the primary market in prison, because the primary market did not exist anymore. The State had brought it to the chopping block, for good. Per new correctional facility directive, issued by the Superintendent, sunglasses of any kind were no longer permitted to be received through the facility package room. Existing pairs in the possession of inmates or those brought into the facility through transfers, were luckily grandfathered in and allowed. Henceforth, no sunglasses allowed in. This had the same effect any abrupt, unannounced supply shock in a market economy would produce: the price of the now-scarce sunglasses shot up. The pair I had paid a paltry eight dollars for could now easily fetch thirty, even forty dollars. This was almost a 500% return on investment (ROI)! Should we reconsider traditional asset classes in here maybe?

The offers were plentiful, and they routinely amazed me. This was not simply for the amusement I derived from the law of supply working at its best, but more from the value the other inmates placed on an intrinsically low-value good. The sunglasses were a luxury good, but one which lacked the traditional quality and durability of a luxury good. These were cheap shades made in some factory in mainland China. They'd been shipped over, rebranded, and sold for eight dollars in a prison mail order catalog. You may ask why all this matters...what's my point? The point is the prison economy is fascinating—not as complex as our larger country's economy, but certainly more interesting.

The economy inside the fence is still governed by micro and macro economic forces; it still operates under the laws of supply and demand and in line with most modern economic theory. The system is a rude marriage between an antiquated barter economy and a more traditional currency-centric framework of exchange. Many transactions take place with a simple exchange or trade of goods, after a rudimentary and inaccurate assignment of value. Resultant market inefficiencies abound. Increasingly, exchanges are made using prison currency: hard cash, which in here is postal stamps. These come in one denomination: Forty-four cents. A second, slightly less liquid currency that is acceptable tender is tobacco. Both tenders hold the same tripartite function as the Greenback does in our economy outside the fence: as a medium of exchange, a store of value and as a unit of account.

Do black markets exist on *the inside* too? Are illicit trades thriving? Is fast money still attractive in the *big house*? Well, of course it is! These are the people who made the rackets on the streets work, those who made them thrive. They just happened to be unlucky enough to get pinched, or were too amateurish to evade the heat. They've been relegated from the Majors to the Pop-Warner league, from kilos to shots of coffee, from stacks of Benjamins to rolls of postal flags. But the mentality remains, the modus operandi endures, and the tragedy continues.

The hustle in here is just like the hustle out there, except the weight has plummeted, and the stakes have multiplied. Where the kitty of illicit monies was once stacks of cash and jewels, it's now a coffer of stamps and Newports. This new, relative wealth is just as transferable, just as powerful and just as corrupting. The ill-gotten proceeds are laundered back into legitimacy, just like on the outside. The stamps and bricks of Newports from the endless rackets are plowed into the legal money supply. This is done through the purchase of inmate artwork, haircuts, food from packages from the street, and other legal procurements.

This is not to say a legal, formal and sanctioned economy does not exist in prison, because it does and it must. It simply rides bitch to the more urgent and relevant market for illicit necessaries. These are the rackets that feed the ravenous and never-ending hunger of human vice, vice in such concentration—in such close and exceeding quarter—it is overwhelming in its tragedy.

There is access to regular monies in prison, to an account denoted in U.S. Greenbacks. It's not all stamps and tobacco, and more than simply quid pro quo. Each of us has an inmate account maintained by the Office of Inmate Accounts. This is an account which receives our state wages as direct deposits, and which our families can send money to as well. We then are able to disburse funds for the purchase of legal, permissible things, such as goods and supplies from the commissary every two weeks, items from outside mail order vendors, for legal copies and other such things.

Just as in the broader world, there are some inmates who transact entirely within the legal economy. These people never venture into the risk and reward of the illicit. But unlike out there, they are the minority in here. The vast majority of inmates in prison find themselves squarely planted in the realm of the unlawful. Some may straddle both worlds, but most reside in the latter.

Enter the curious character of a certain inmate I knew named Giacotti. Giacotti was already at this facility when I got here. He'd been in this dorm and jail for a while, over three years. He was one of the leading, if not *the* most successful, entrepreneurs in the facility. He was industrious, resourceful and reliable. When you needed something, you went to Giacotti. From a Twinkie to a twelve-inch shank, he could procure the item within 24 hours tops. That is, if he didn't have it in stock already, in his seemingly bottomless locker. His locker was like a turn-of-the-century general store, no exaggeration. This is why he is so unique...why his decisions, his operations, his entire identity, exemplify the micro and macro dynamics of the prison economy.

Giacotti was originally from a small town in southern Italy, about an hour and a half south of Naples, on the western coast of Italy abutting the Mediterranean. He was born there, but his family moved to Brooklyn when he was young. His roots and his loyalties remained with the Old World, and you were constantly reminded of this. You were also reminded, most contrary to custom, of his affiliation with La Cosa Nostra. His family had a lock on the Bedford Stuyvesant area of Brooklyn, supposedly. I wasn't about to question this claim, and no one else seemed eager to, either. Giacotti wasn't merely intimidating through his connections, through his supposed "Made" status (although that was most of it), it was because he was physically intimidating as well. He stood six foot four and weighed probably 240. And that 240 was rock solid muscle. The guy spent over three hours working out in the weight pit every day, religiously.

Giacotti represented the underworld. He symbolized the black market and the realm of the illicit, the unauthorized economy that dominated prison. He had his hand in almost every racket known to corrections. From his main hustle as loan shark, to price-gouged food and supply sales, to the tobacco hustle, to the illicit marijuana and heroin trade, to protection, contracts, even package fraud. He was in everything. He was like the Warren Buffet of the disallowed. Giacotti ran a wholly proscribed agglomeration of business interests in prison, akin to Berkshire Hathaway, in a very distant way. Giacotti followed a value investing approach, and sought fundamental prowess and intrinsic value over the speculation of growth. He was a true entrepreneur, one who would surely be a multimillionaire at liberty were it not for his poor choice of the maturing industry of crime—an industry where the first-mover advantage of the early racketeers had already waned, leaving only a trail of RICO jetsam in remote locales.

So we're brought to Giacotti's primary racket: good, old-fashioned loan sharking. This was his most lucrative hustle, where he could earn the largest margins in the coveted return-on-capital financial metric.

It seems to never go out of style with the wise guys, or even with the wannabe wise guys. The demand for quick cash by unqualified debtors is always healthy, and it's always inelastic. The elasticity is so low because of the very immediacy and urgency of this type of demand. This need is only magnified in prison, when ramifications for delinquent accounts payable can be swift and extremely violent.

Drug debts are the most common. A few past-due payments can immediately result in a contract for physical harm being taken out on the debtor. You don't get a collection agency writing and calling in prison, you get a group of thugs beating the shit out of you, moving you quickly back to fiscal responsibility and credit discipline. This threat is precisely what drives the inelasticity of this type of demand, and where Giacotti comes into the picture.

When an addict's habit overwhelms his ability to finance the addiction, he goes to Giacotti. Giacotti will essentially buy the debt owed the dealer. Then he'll charge the addict (debtor) an insanely usurious rate of interest on the loan, much higher than he may have originally had. Right now, prevailing market forces have settled the rate at one hundred per cent if repaid within two weeks. After this, it jumps from two-to-one up to three-to-one, or two hundred percent. If the debt remains unpaid after a month from Giacotti's assumption, he himself will take out another contract on the hapless addict/debtor. This victim, unfortunately, will then usually leave the jail on a stretcher, with his face cut up from a razor attack, to forever be reminded of his debt, his addiction...and Giacotti.

After usury, the drug trade itself is probably the next most lucrative racket in corrections. The thing with the drug trade is that it carries much, much more risk than any other racket. The reward is high, but not commensurate with the risk assumed. If caught in the act of smuggling drugs, in the possession of them or the actual transfer or sale of them, the inmate is brought to outside civilian court for new charges. These are almost always new felony charges, which also means more time. This is why Giacotti kept his distance from this racket. This is why he kept layers of insulation between him and the foot soldiers, so to speak.

Now he was involved—don't get it twisted—but he was more of a silent partner. He was more passive angel investor than active manager. More of a Chairman and less of a CEO. He would bankroll operations, front the money and put people up in business. Giacotti negotiated brutal terms for any party willing to assent to his offer and accept his verbal contract.

Then there was the relatively benign hustle of the food and supply trade. The provision juggle, as some might call it. Giacotti had a convenience store in his locker. He had every food item and cosmetic product in demand one could conjure. Ho-Ho's, Jolly Ranchers, Pop Tarts, canned foods, pastries, soda, soaps, lotions, shampoos. Everything one might need to hold him over until his next commissary or package. The catch? Everything was two-for-one. Meaning you "borrow" a bottle of shampoo for three days until you got to the commissary, and when you come back from the commissary, you had better have two bottles for Giacotti or there were gonna be problems, consequences very much worth avoiding.

Then there was the protection racket, one that has seen its market share in the organized crime gamut wane in recent years. Gangs have risen in power; more have organized and unionized, if you will, around common interests. The demand has fallen, but the hustle nonetheless remains profitable. Giacotti had people, he had muscle other than those that draped his skeleton in a heavy curtain, and Giacotti had clients. He had clients that paid regular dues, every time, without missing a payment. Of course the majority of the protection was sold as insurance against an embellished, if not totally fictitious, threat. But then again, when the hell was the threat ever real? When was it ever tangible? Ever pressing? That was the bedrock sales pitch, coupled with a nice delivery by a sales crew who'd make you an offer you couldn't refuse...the emphasis on *couldn't*.

All of these rackets, these hustles, these illicit trades, generated large profits. They all produced hard prison currency, loads and loads of undeclared stamps, cartons of tobacco, durable goods. These were all proceeds that needed to be hidden from the authorities and laundered into legitimacy or else they'd be seized, and all would be for naught. You'd then only be left with a long stretch in solitary confinement, and possibly new charges to contemplate the age-old aphorism "crime doesn't pay."

Giacotti and others like him had a solution to this problem, like they always did. It's amazing what the criminal mind is capable of; how productive and accomplished it could be, if put to good use and not wasted on the circumvention of law, order and morality. Giacotti needed a way to keep his dirty money from the authorities; he needed a way to keep his luxury purchases with said ill-gotten proceeds on the low. This was difficult, and much more so than on the outside.

In this near-Orwellian atmosphere, Big Brother's ubiquity is astonishing. The State has a uniformed eye on everything, a clandestine ear everywhere. If the agents of the State are not explicitly on the payroll, they're still on the *payroll*. Corrections has long been infiltrated by rodents—by rats, snitches and confidential informants. They're as common as fruit flies. Sooner or later, no matter how careful you are, the pinch will come, just as it did on the street. Only it will hurt more in here. It will seize your conscience like a vice grip, tightening with time and maturing with reflection.

So Giacotti will stash profits in offshore havens. He'll seek out weaker inmates in need to act as private banks of deposit. It was a bit like the way wealthy Americans often look to Switzerland (or at least used to, before the UBS debacle) for private, largely tax-free preservation of their wealth. He may pay nine different people in the dorm five stamps apiece to temporarily hold fifty of his stamps each. This way he doesn't get caught with more than the fifty stamps you're allowed to have in your possession. The cost to him is negligible, given the source of funds and the risk of getting caught. The risk of a bank failure was always present here though. One of those people Giacotti contracted with might unexpectedly go to solitary confinement, they might get transferred...and when something like that happened, there was no FDIC to turn to.

Another way to launder the dirty profits was through the commissary. Giacotti would approach people every day who were going to commissary, and ask them if they were buying stamps. If they were, he'd offer them a deal they couldn't refuse. If you were stupid enough to say yes, you were in business with Giacotti. He'd pay you ten stamps for three dollars in commissary money, meaning he'd pay you a premium equivalent to a dollar and forty cents (.44 X 10 = $4.40 - $3.00 = $1.40 profit). This way he could take down his stamp reserves and at the same time stock up on commissary goods he was just turning around and selling on a two-for-one basis anyhow. Sounds a bit like the secondary mortgage market in America. It was a win-win for him and others like him, and there were others.

We mustn't forget the macroeconomic dynamics that provide the environment to enable these microeconomic transactions to take place the way they do. Like the country's larger economy, the correctional economy operates in much the same way. It is subject to many of the same forces and laws of economics we've come to know as making up the body of classical economic theory. Many of the same institutional forces are at work behind the fences, just on a much smaller scale. For example, our Federal Reserve in prison is the security establishment apparatus. The security institution of the prison industrial complex is chartered with two of the same mandates as the U.S. Federal Reserve: keep inmate unemployment low and keep the level of inflation low. Levels above historically natural rates in either category can lead to serious structural friction in the prison economy, friction that can quickly turn to widespread violence, unrest and even riot.

Maybe the money supply has ballooned, and the M1 macroeconomic metric is way above the market-clearing equilibrium. This is caused by the multiplier effect and is compounded by capital inflows—foreign direct investment (FDI)—into the prison economy from the outside economy. The barriers to entry are exceedingly high, but the tariff on goods and monies imported is zero. This is causing prices to rise, and inflation is getting out of control. This leads to more criminal activity, more discontent and more violence. The facility's Security must act. Their own FOMC convenes. The Chairman (Deputy Superintendent of Security) lobbies and persuades attending brass to initiate a facility-wide shakedown. The over-supply of currency in the market (excess stamps, tobacco, et cetera) is driving increased drug activity. Gangs are moving weight before prices go up and demand ebbs, if only slightly.

Monetary policy must be amended, or tweaked at the very least. A round of initial quantitative tightening must be commenced at once. The squad gears up and the uniforms are assembled; the brass convenes, and the platoon moves out. The dorms are descended upon randomly. An ambuscade of sorts ensues. The units are ravished. The lockers and their contents are torn apart, belongings strewn without care. The mission is singular in nature, the objective clear in purpose: search and seize all illicit contraband, with an emphasis on hard currency stores. Excess stamps, tobacco, allowed provisions...take it all. No mercy for personal property.

The tools of the Federal Reserve's counterpart in prison are a bit different, as one can imagine. There is no control over the Federal Funds Rate, there is no room or mechanism to manipulate the short term interest rate of the prison economy. The only real and effective tool is the open market operations available, such as the aforesaid round of quantitative tightening. This served its purpose wonderfully. The facility-wide shakedown netted huge reserves of illicit proceeds, and sent several inmates to solitary confinement. It also accomplished the larger, macroeconomic objective: It reduced the facility's illicit money supply considerably, which in no time would ease inflationary pressures. This would in turn quell the rising yard activity and accompanying violence. It had succeeded.

Fed Chairman Bernanke would be proud of his correctional likeness.

Giacotti escaped Big Brother's porous dragnet—its loose colander—this time. He was lucky and he knew it. He was visibly anxious after this last sweep. He knew his organization was becoming too large, the operation too big to remain off the fuzz's radar for much longer. He had become prison-rich in here. He was one of the lead ballers on the compound. Giacotti had the flyest new shoes, dozens of them. He had all the new clothes—the Polos, Lacoste, all of it. He ate three prepared meals a day from his paid chef. He had his dishes done promptly after meals. He had all his other services subcontracted: cube cleaning, ironing, laundry, weight gathering in the pit before he worked out. You name it, Giacotti hired it out. He was just doing what any intelligent businessman would, as any deft entrepreneur who knew anything about the basic economic concept of opportunity cost.

Giacotti knew the value of his time. He knew that time is money, and he knew his time was best spent conducting or expanding his business interests. It was better spent cultivating or founding new going concerns. If he wasted his time on the menial support of his burgeoning lifestyle, his day would be almost consumed by it. That's the level of largesse he'd achieved...the grandeur his ripe coffers had provided. He had the wherewithal to focus on his core competencies—his key businesses and main profit centers. He had to keep his vertically and horizontally integrated franchise afloat. After all, he was the sole proprietor. There was no limited liability company in prison, he was fully liable for all debts incurred.

Giacotti would continue his business operations. His empire was still afloat, but its buoyancy was waning. He was firmly established in the mature industry of crime, the riskiest and most volatile of all industries. The climate was always hostile and the risks almost always far exceeded the rewards. He persevered nevertheless, but not like he once did...before the latest sweep. The crackdown had jostled Giacotti. It had shaken his resolve, and even penetrated his rhino skin a bit. He knew the long odds of not getting pinched in the game he was in. He'd been doing this his whole life, and he'd been paying for this his whole life. He'd been paying for what he had done with his life and with his time. And he remembered, time was money. This is what upset him most.

Giacotti was finally realizing that crime doesn't in fact pay. He would have a good run on the streets, for maybe four, even five, years, and then he'd get pinched and sent away to do twice that amount of time behind bars. Sure he'd lived like Riley, but then he'd live like the McCourts. He was finally understanding the trade-off, and how the brief stints of pecuniary excess would blind him to the sunk costs of an inevitable stretch in the slammer. He couldn't keep doing this, it wasn't worth it. He was thirty-nine. This was his fourth state prison sentence. He had thirteen felony arrests on his rap sheet. He'd been in and out of detention centers, jails and institutions since he was sixteen. He was getting tired.

Over the coming months, Giacotti began to change. Slowly at first, but it happened. He started by receding from the drug trade almost entirely. Then he began to pull out of the connected bastion of the protection racket, the extortion hustle. These were simply too risky. There were too many snitches with loose lips, too many confidential informants working for the State. He stayed in loan sharking though. He had to, it was his bread and butter. This was his stalwart producer. He couldn't give up all the luxury he so lavishly enjoyed. Hell, change was hard. Change took time, especially for a gangster like Giacotti, one so affected with hubris and self-inflation, he practically had no reflective abilities. He had no real way of connecting character frailty to life folly.

As he pulled out of markets, young opportunists entered in his absence. This always happened when market vacancies arose, both in the legal environs and in those not so legal landscapes. When a member in the economic ecology of a market vanished, the demand didn't vanish with him. The demand stayed, and it shone with a luster that rarely went unnoticed. There were always others to fill the void and meet the market demand. This was the same in both the real world and in prison; it was the same in the realm of the legal and the prohibited. The labor supply curve was steep. It was treacherous like a sharp descent down a backcountry basin. But inelasticity had no reservation, and it skied like Bode Miller.

Life went on though. Drugs were still available, goods were still procurable and loans and tobacco still within reach. All of this was available for a price, the point of value where a transaction can be consummated; the exact point where two consenting parties can come together as buyer and seller of a good or service and exchange, for the mutual benefit of both. This is the definition of market efficiency—when all parties have perfect knowledge and mobility, and are free from government constraint to contract and transact as they see fit.

Giacotti never did get pinched, at least while he was at this facility living in my dorm. He was transferred shortly after the big shakedown to Woodbourne Correctional Facility, which was closer to the City in Ulster County. He said before he left he was going to get out of the game when he went home. He talked of how the life wasn't for him anymore, how he couldn't come back to prison again, no matter what. The guys on the dorm talked of him long after he left. Mostly out of envy...reverence...respect for his business acumen and his pecuniary prowess. They also complained. It sucked losing the convenience store that was his locker. No more late night Nutty Buddy Bar buys, no more quick cash, no more arsenal sales, no more dealmaker.

People adjusted, and they found what they needed elsewhere. Often this was now for a higher price and after a longer wait, another consequence of the supply shock Giacotti's departure created. Things will even out though, and a new equilibrium will settle. The curves always find a point of commonality, where conflicting forces can agree to simply chill out for a minute, settle down and let the masses transact. The institution moved forward, as it always does. It went on in perpetuity, like the Great American Corporation. As the larger U.S. economy chugged along behind the locomotive tow of corporate earnings and consumer spending, so too did the U.S. correctional economy behind the illicit tow of human vice and weakness. This was just like it always had been, and as it probably always will be.

ON CHOW

It was a cold and dark night. The westerly gale blew across the treeless yard with no inhibition, no sympathy. But you had only yourself to blame if you weren't prepared. You only had to peer out of the thick paned windows in the dorm to see, to notice how there was not one tree, shrub or structure capable of weakening those wearisome westerlies as they tore across the barren expanse. But this was entirely seasonal, to be expected and planned on. The autumnal segue to winter had begun, taking many of the weight pit's fainthearted with it. This was a good thing; it's what us true weightlifting loyalists waited patiently for all year.

There were about twenty people in the entire weight pit, where only a month ago it had been double, maybe triple that. I relished these nights, where I knew I wouldn't have to take my mark by the dormitory's gate like an institutionalized steed, waiting for the recreation call so I could dash out and be the first to the weight pit. So I could rush around and gather all the barbells and dumbbells I needed before the others descended, before they hoarded and said no.

My workout partner Josh wasn't as committed as I was; he was still a bit of a work-in-progress. Don't get me wrong, he was a good workout partner, but I had always worked out solo prior to our partnership. I had no real benchmark from which I could gauge his performance. I just knew he strolled out to the yard when they called the recreation-run…cigarette in hand, and no urgency in his step. This is what frustrated me.

Tonight we were doing our chest routine, my favorite routine of the week. This meant it was Sunday, and there were even fewer people than the otherwise depleted ranks on this cold November evening. This was because tonight was Sunday Night Football. It was week ten of a contentious season, and the Giants had a big game. We had everything we needed, an over-abundance really, of old rusted iron masses to aid in the chiseling of our frames. We were going heavy this particular week. I was under the oppression of a two-hundred-and-forty pound barbell on the bench press, pressing it up for the sixth and last rep when I heard my name, shouted from across the mostly empty weight pit. It was Bobby; I knew it before I even looked up.

Bobby used to be in my dorm when he first got to Cayuga Correctional Facility earlier that year. He had come from a maximum-security facility not far from here, Five Points Correctional. His security classification had finally fallen to medium, four years into his lengthy sentence. Bobby had 9-27 years to muse over the risk-reward ratio of a string of successively disturbing burglaries. These were larcenies committed in the drug induced stupor of a six-day crack binge...all to support the continuing bender that was approaching cardiac arrest, but would settle this time for physical arrest by the authorities.

What was even more unsettling was the fact that this was Bobby's fifth state prison term. This was the adjudicated coup de grace that would effectively ferry him into old age, behind the fence and away from his family and loved ones, again. When he talked about his crimes—about his partying—he did so in jest. He tried to laugh and poke fun, but you could tell he was rotting away inside. Bobby was forced to put forth the weathered and stoic facade required by the penitentiary. He was encouraged to deflect blame to others, to the system, to avoid responsibility for his crimes and his addiction. Weakness, emotions and sentimentality were forbidden in prison. If anyone knew this, it was Bobby from his thirty years in and out of the system.

"Listen, I got something I thought you might be interested in. They just added something new to the breakfast menu, permanently. They're replacing raisins with walnuts, starting with tomorrow morning's oatmeal. So I'm selling a latex glove's worth of walnuts for five stamps. Either of you guys interested?" Bobby asked, as a smile emerged in anticipation.

Josh and I looked at each other, and smiled. This wasn't the first time Bobby had offered to sell some commodity out of the mess hall; he got a job there for that exact reason. That was his main hustle in here, aside from his occasional tobacco trade in the yard. The problem was Bobby's addiction from the streets wasn't in remission, and he sure as hell wasn't in recovery. He was simply abstinent from one substance, his drug of choice, crack-cocaine. He now substituted tobacco and coffee where the crack rock had left off, and his appetite was just as ravenous and demanding of his means.

I tended to refrain from any illicit trade on the black market in prison. I did this out of principle and out of fear of the ever-present informant, who lurked behind almost every dark corner of transaction in here, it seemed. I looked at Josh, who seemed to be on the same page.

"You know what, Bobby, I think we're good. We're going to have to pass," I said in response.

"I knew it! Why wouldn't you pass up a great opportunity to get a bag of walnuts?" he said with a bit of pointed sarcasm as he turned to leave our area, without the answer he wanted and the five stamps he thought certain.

"Well, let me know if you change your mind— which you probably won't—but let me know if you do, because I got boatloads of nuts now," Bobby said, as he faded back into his routine across the weight pit and we began to resume ours.

"You're up," I said to Josh, as he laid down on the bench, two-hundred-and-forty pounds towering with authority eighteen inches above his face.

"I'm going for eight reps," Josh said as I lifted the weight off the rack and ceded it to him.

"Of course, you always gotta try and exceed me, right?" I said as he began to rep the set.

The next morning arrived quickly. There was an unusual air of anticipation floating around the dorm. The novelty of the new nuts on the breakfast menu had created a stir, and had sparked a larger awakening of the normally sleeping masses at this hour. The new jacks on the dormitory waited eagerly by the door for the officer to call the morning chow run. The old timers knew better. This new foodstuff fad would be fleeting, simply another whim of the food service administrator. Here today, gone tomorrow. These guys knew not to get excited about much of anything in here. It was always better to keep an even keel—subscribe to the ancient philosophy of stoicism—than to indulge and later suffer. Expectations can't be dashed if you don't have any, and nowhere else is this more true than in prison.

The chow call finally came and the floodgates opened, deluging the walkway tributaries with a sea of unfamiliar faces, as the flow of state green merged into the main current headed south toward the Mess Hall. Everyone was walking fast, really fast, like they were handing out sentence time cuts instead of walnuts. I was lost somewhere in the middle of the flow. I entered the Mess Hall with the usual step up, my shiny state boots greeting the focused stare of the Boot Police on duty that morning. The same officer was always checking to make sure everyone's boots were tied and properly laced. You'd be surprised how many had effectively turned their high-backed boots into open-backed sandals. They were quickly and routinely pulled over and scolded. Sometimes they were issued tickets, sometimes they were even sent back to the dorm...with no walnuts, mad as hell.

The wide flow of inmates channeled back into a narrow file following the perimeter of the cavernous Mess Hall. The floors looked wet, but it was just the countless hours spent by porters buffing away. The ceiling was lined with yet another dizzying array of blinding fluorescents. I squinted to adjust as I followed the single file line toward the food. As I approached the assembly line of food servers with my brown plastic tray, I noticed it: the scoop they were using for the walnuts was different than the one used for the raisins. It was not the six-ounce scoop like it said on the posted menu. This scoop was tiny. It couldn't be more than two ounces, but it was supposed to be a one-for-one swap—walnuts for raisins, same quantity.

"What the hell? We're gettin' screwed here?" I said to the man next to me, in disbelief.

Immediately it dawned on me: Bobby! That son of a bitch! He must have sold so many gloves of walnuts over the last week that he was forced to pay off the line server to use a smaller scooper, so his cover wouldn't be blown when they did the food inventory. That bastard! He'd singlehandedly taken the walnut cache down so far that he was now fucking the rest of us, just so he wouldn't get busted. He was doing this just so he wouldn't get thrown in solitary confinement, his racket unstrung and his hustle halted. And this wasn't the first time this had happened. Mess Hall rackets by kitchen workers were commonplace in prison, to the constant chagrin of the nonpaying general population of inmates who wouldn't cough up stamps for extra state food, no matter how novel or in what volume. But you could do nothing.

Kitchen workers managed to smuggle the craziest things out of the Mess Hall, in shocking quantity, and right past the tight border security at the Mess Hall threshold. They'd steal full five-pound packs of cold cuts, twelve-inch stacks of cheese, cake batter by the boatload, icing, bags of spices and seasonings, and various other eats. I don't know how they did it. The usual drug mule modus operandi was out of the question, the human cavity "stow-away" not an option, as sheer size and material smuggled disqualified it. To this day it's still a mystery how they get all that food out of the Mess Hall. Sometimes I wonder if, by nature, it simply had to be an inside job.

The Great Walnut Letdown was soon forgotten, as most other routine, mundane things were in prison. At the end of the day, it was just another meal, just one with not as many walnuts now. But it was still just a meal. It was still just a way to divide the day into thirds to get through it quicker. Prison is the only place in the world where time is not an asset. It is the only place where it is not a valued commodity held above all others. Time in prison is a liability. The more you have, the worse the balance sheet of your life looks. Like a dentist or proctologist appointment, prison is one of those rare things in life to be gotten through as quickly as possible.

Back on the dormitory unit the deal making had already commenced for the evening meal. They were serving liver as the main course, accompanied by a lovely baked potato with faux-butter, set alongside a rancid portion of the worst smelling cabbage imaginable, and adorned with one six-ounce carton of chocolate milk to wash it all down. And for the finale—and the only reason I even went to this meal—they had vanilla cake with chocolate frosting. I had to hit the State Comestible Exchange trading floor before it was too late; I had to start working the room before the limited supply of willing cake sellers had liquidated or bartered away their one allotted piece.

The recreation room before a meal was like the Chicago Mercantile Exchange before the closing bell. Bids would fly through the air, asks were shouted across loud throngs of people. It was akin to a true commodities trading pit, a place where buyers and sellers converged and looked to transact. Immediacy and the price inelasticity of demand for certain menu favorites often made this a seller's market. There were even arbitrage opportunities, as some deft market specialists—also known as seasoned convicts—would buy in one circle and then immediately sell in another for a profit, exploiting the often imperfect knowledge of market participants. Sometimes they'd harvest profits of up to one hundred percent of their original outlay. As an economics guy, it was fascinating.

Others might strictly operate in the barter market. This is where I preferred to transact. I'd move in and out of Mess Hall conversations I might overhear as I walked around the recreation room, seemingly unawares.

"Chicken patty for cake, I got a chicken patty for cake," I might hear.

I'd keep it moving, I wanted cake too, wrong market.

"Tater tots for pudding, taters for pudding." Damn it, wrong again.

"I got cake tonight for the meatloaf tomorrow," I hear.

"Right here! Right here! I'll take that," I yell to the asking party, as I approach him to hit the hammer and seal the deal.

"You got it. Find me on the walkway tonight, and don't forget the meatloaf for tomorrow's lunch," he says.

"I won't, don't worry. I got you," I say as I spin off in search of another piece of cake for the right trade. My sweet tooth was driving my behavior, plus I despised liver.

As we headed to evening chow that night, I had to coordinate the caravan. I ended up procuring three pieces of cake, in addition to my own. A little ridiculous, you might think. A sugar glutton, you say? Maybe, but what can I say? As the dorm inhabitants moved closer to the Mess Hall, almost like a voracious pride approaching its prey, I went to great lengths to keep together my contingent of cake sellers. It's hard though to be a community organizer in prison. This is no place for a leader or the face of a cause, even if that cause is just the consumption of four pieces of vanilla cake covered with chocolate frosting.

I had everyone lined up by the time we reached the door to the Mess Hall. We were greeted by the establishment's maitre d'hôtel, and he wasn't your typical maitre d'hôtel. He wore a white shirt, yes, but it was adorned with correctional caparisons. He also had the power to deny you a table and a meal, and unfortunately, you couldn't simply go down the street to another restaurant. I made sure my boots were tied, my shirt tucked in and hat off. I also made sure my business partners followed suit. I wanted every piece of cake I contracted for.

As we slowly made our way around the Mess Hall's perimeter, I wondered how the slop would actually be tonight, but I mainly focused on the cake. I hope the Mess Hall workers had a good day, I thought to myself. I hope they were feeling generous—even profligate— in the icing of the large sheets of semi-cooked Cisco cake batter. If they were, my transactions would in fact prove to be good investments. If not, I'd simply have to eat the loss, literally. I might even be forced to reevaluate my trading strategy, possibly shift my focus to a less risky asset class. Maybe I should transact in bagels, or waffles, or even apple crisp. These were dishes that were less susceptible to quality fluctuations—in other words, harder to fuck up.

When we got close enough to see the sheet of cake glisten under the blemish-unveiling fluorescence, I rejoiced. The cake looked moist and the frosting plentiful! Life was good, but for a moment! The liver, however, looked dubious, which is precisely why I traded it away for the grilled cheese later in the week. The other side dishes looked different, too. For one, the baked potato was about the size of a lemon, and the cabbage was being scooped with noticeable reservation. We all looked at each other, exchanged a few words, then looked at the kitchen worker in bewilderment. His eyebrows slowly rose from the flat roof of an indifferent expression, to the stark peak of an A-Frame in similar wonder. We all knew what it was, and were equally powerless to stop its manifestation.

The state's budget woes had managed to creep into the already dismal state provender. Come on, you gotta be kidding me, I thought! First the red ink was felt in the toilet paper. The rolls seemed to shrink by about a centimeter in width almost overnight. This made the sheets just narrow enough to not fully cover the rim of the toilet seat, requiring now double the expenditure of precious TP handed out only once a week. Awesome. Then it was seen in the envelope allotment, which went from unlimited to five envelopes a week. Great. And now it was being experienced firsthand in the Mess Hall meals. Wonderful.

As I approached the cake station of the food assembly line, I realized I knew the guy serving the cake. Nice, I thought, added bonus! I'll now get the best pieces on the sheet. As I move from on-deck to the plate, I see the next piece in line on the oversized sheet is a sparsely iced corner piece. Of course, why wouldn't it be? I guess my luck at the Mess Hall Roulette table had finally expired. But I had an out. I had one last shot at a good piece to complete the dessert quadrilateral: the croupier clad in kitchen white with spatula in hand. His name was Zach, and I knew him from working out in the weight pit.

Our eyes met at the perfect time. He saw my discontent with the awaiting runt-of-a-piece. He glanced slowly to his left. The station officer was chatting with one of the Mess Hall civilians. He moved the spatula to the next row, and thrust it directly under the centermost piece. This piece was at the cake's highest, and at the icing's deepest. He placed it in its awaiting compartment on the plastic tray I held in front of me. I smiled, nodded my head slightly in a show of gratitude, and kept it moving to avoid detection.

I followed the train of inmates past the Butter Police, past the Spoon Police, and over to my designated steel stool on the long stainless steel table. My partners and I exchanged our food, and I now had four beautifully appointed pieces of cake sitting in front of me, waiting to be consumed. As I began to eat my large dessert for dinner, I noticed the usual table antics taking place. Latex fingers from a cleaning glove are carefully brought from the shade of a pocket into view. Plastic fingers filled with all kinds of seasonings, obscure seasoning mixtures I'd never heard of until I came to prison. Sazon? Adobo? Whatever happened to basil, and sage? The guy across from me flopped out an old state bread bag, glanced smoothly over both shoulders to see where the officers were looking, and then shoveled every last thing from his tray into the bag. He skillfully threw the bag down the front of his half-zipped jacket, and got up and left.

I felt stuffed after those four pieces. I may have overdone it this time, I thought. I knew I only needed two, but I didn't like the liver, or the side dishes for that matter, and I didn't feel like cooking myself back at the "shelter." Although the food in prison is about as bland and uneventful as bad hospital fare or old US Airways repast from the nineties, it is at least somewhat nutritionally balanced. Well, for the most part anyway. The state operates on a statewide eight-week menu that's been devised by the department's own internal Office of Nutrition in the capital. So we can hope at least some thought's gone into it. There is variety, and a mixture of nourishment. But the problem is the foodstuffs are heavily slanted toward the carb-rich foods such as bread, pasta, rice and potatoes. When coupled with the general inactivity of a large segment of the general inmate population in here, this explains much of the higher than average rates of obesity in prison.

The good thing was you had the option to cook your own meals on the dormitory units. You could cook in the two microwaves provided in each dorm, if you were fortunate enough to have the means with which to buy food through the commissary or have food sent in through the package room. Some people never even stepped foot in the Mess Hall. They refused to eat the state fare, out of principle or luxury, or both. Some people never missed a meal, usually out of pure necessity. Most fell somewhere in the middle, and would congregate under the center of the bell curve. As the old adage goes, all the work gets done in the center. As in life, so in prison.

I fell right in the middle of that comfortable majority. I would attend the mess hall every morning largely for the two cartons of milk they served. They would also rotate meals among bagels, waffles, pancakes and Egg-Beaters. Oh yeah, and French toast every four weeks, which was a favorite, and quite the correctional treat. I enjoyed this variety, plus it was hard to botch a breakfast, for the most part. Lunch and dinner I attended less regularly, and grew more dependent on my own personal store of rations, and desire to go through the rigmarole of cooking full meals in a microwave.

My cooking usually fell on occasions. I'd cook when I got my commissary purchase every two weeks, when I'd binge on pizza and wings for two days. I'd have four meals of pizza and wings in less than forty-eight hours. Then I'd swear off the two until the next commissary buy came around, when I'd order the same quantity again. I was also a big fan of the simple and underrated sandwich. And of course, holidays were always a time for a big food production. The preparation and gathering of the right foods was something that sometimes took weeks in advance, like for this Thanksgiving, for instance.

They called me down to the package room to receive my food package the week before Thanksgiving—a Wednesday morning. We had deliberately ordered the delicatessen delights the week prior, to ensure they arrived on time. The package room was notorious for sitting on processed packages for days before they actually called you down to pick it up. I didn't want to take the chance of having the food delivered to me on the Friday after Thanksgiving.

I brought my large net bag down to the package room to carry my food back to the dorm. I was the first in a long queue of inmates picking up similar holiday provisions. I wasn't here to waste time, in any regard.

"Weimer. Package for inmate Weimer," the package room supervisor said, as he placed the seemingly pilfered remainder of my package on the counter.

"You're over your thirty-five pound limit for food weight for the month. Your last food package last weekend was twenty-eight pounds, and this one's thirteen. What do you want to do with the items over weight?" Officer Milton asked me, as my mood changed instantly.

"You've gotta be kidding me, officer. There's no way that last package was over twenty-five pounds," I said, visibly annoyed.

"Do I look like I'm kidding? Do I? What are you going to do with the denied items? Send them home at your expense? Donate them? Or destroy them?" he asked me again.

I couldn't believe it, it was happening again. It was always something with this package room. I'd never received a package without some denial, hold-up, or issue to resolve. Never. And now I was left with effectively one option: the first option, send the stuff to my father so at least he could enjoy it. The other two options—donate or destroy—would end up with the same end result: in the back of one of the package room officer's pickup trucks, and later on his dining room table. And I wasn't about to let that happen.

"Officer Milton, sir, can you please make an exception? It's the holiday season. I need this food for the meal I'm putting together. Can you please make an exception?" I entreated.

He stared at me. A moment or two passed. He was clearly contemplating, considering my request.

"Do you have any Snickers candy bars?" he finally replied.

I was shocked, thought I'd misheard him. Was he soliciting a bribe? A candy bribe? I wouldn't put it past him. It had certainly happened before here; these environs weren't exactly ethical epicenters. Graft was commonplace in prison; I'd just never been a party to it.

"Uhhhh...not on me, sir, but I have a ten-pack of Snickers Mini's in my locker. I can run back to the dorm and get them and be back in two minutes," I replied with interest.

Again a moment passes.

"That's not gonna work. It's COD here, gotta come prepared. Better luck next time. Now what are you gonna do with the denied items for the last time?" he asked.

You gotta be kidding me! I was that close!

"I have to send them home, I guess. Option one," I told him.

He hands me the form, and I fill out the necessary info. I option, address and sign. He takes the form, slips it back into my file, and pushes the bin full of food toward me. I take it and proceed wearily to the plaintive package periphery, where I'll soon be joined by the others whose holiday hopes have also been dashed.

As I place the depleted container down, I realize one high point in all of this: he didn't deny the pièce de résistance: I got both of the three-pound chickens! These were the central component to our Thanksgiving meal. Well that was good at least, because they basically denied everything else. I swear they must have that scale they use calibrated wrong on purpose. Or they press the *Tare* button no matter the size or weight of the packaging, which isn't part of the thirty-five pound food allotment per month. But once again, I am powerless against the authorities. I must roll with the punches, and just remember the Snickers next time.

Now we basically had everything we needed for our holiday production, save a few lesser side items. I was cooking this year with two guys from my dorm. One was my workout partner, Josh, and the other was a guy named Bob. We were each committing different elements to the meal. At present, it stood to be a feast of sorts: two birds, five traditional side dishes, three pies, and all the typical garnishments. These productions and occasional epicurean indulgences helped to numb the pain from being away from our families, for yet another year...in this miasmic wasteland.

Holidays are difficult times in prison. The congregation of family and friends at home, and our looming absence, is tough to simply ignore, but we do what we can. We stay strong and we look ahead. We look to the time when we will return to our seat at the table...to the table of our family, and to the table of society. Hopefully as different individuals; as men who've changed, men who've realized the folly of their ways, and men who've committed to their recovery from them.

So life goes on, as it always does. We'll have a good meal, a nice treat and a welcome respite from the usual state fare and routine. On the outside, life centers on food. At its most base level, we need food to survive and keep living. But food also serves so many other important roles in our lives. It brings us together. It brings families together, friends together, couples and lovers together. It unites and forges bonds. Food also serves as a centerpiece to the society of our peers. It serves as an activity around which we get to know each other better, exchange ideas and opinions, and share our life experiences and what's important to us. Food is crucial to existence, to culture, to society, to survival.

We all sit down and get ready to indulge in the feast we've prepared. Josh looks tired, but focused and ready for the meal ahead. Bob is smiling like a child on Christmas morning, not someone facing down another sixteen Thanksgivings in prison. I'm feeling relaxed and at peace with things. This is my last Thanksgiving in prison, away from my family.

Bob says a short but powerful prayer, and then we dig in. The bird is passed around, the several side dishes exchanged, and the plates begin to pile high. There is a solidarity about our embrace of this meal, yet an understanding that it means something different to each of us.

"Wow," Josh said, as he looks at me and Bob, "Fuckin' lovely chicken here, but what I'd give to be looking at my little girl instead of your ugly mugs."

THE LIFE OF A LIFER

It was a typical fall day in Upstate New York, and then came the shift, from behind the ridge. It moved with a certain foreboding haste, with characteristic resolve from the uncertainty of the West. The sky faded in spectrum above, from light to dark as the clouds moved in. Back in the dorm, the prisoners were largely unaware of the impending storm. The oppressive glow from the countless fluorescent lights obscured any perception of the outside world. If the power of the institution wasn't at fault, it was usually the absence of any real attention given to the "now." The collective mind in prison seemed to straddle the present—one foot planted squarely in the past, and one firmly in the future. This would make any particular moment in the present most significant for that which it did not contain.

The officer called the "Mail" right on schedule. Three-thirty, every afternoon. The usual scurry to the officer's station ensued. It ebbed within minutes; a slow mail day it was. Juan stood up from his steel bunk with noticeable ambivalence. A part of him wanted to sprint to the officer's station, and tear open the envelope he knew was waiting for him. His other, more practical side told him to turn and run in the opposite direction; it told him to flee as far as he could from this long-awaited moment. He headed slowly for the officer's desk. He was worried, didn't know how what to expect. Would they do it to him again, he thought? Could they? When he arrived, he was the only one left with any mail.

"You must be Martinez then, right?" the officer asked.

"Yes, that's right," he offered in reply.

"Big blue envelope, huh? Looks like the moment of truth. Well good luck," he said as he handed Juan the envelope.

Good luck? Good luck! What did this guy mean, good luck? Was the officer being ingenuous or guileful? This cop had to know how slim the odds of parole are. He knew exactly what was in that envelope; he'd seen the same letters every day of his career. A parole denial meant job security for this officer. Well fuck it if he was making a go at him, he didn't care. If he had the answer he so desperately needed in that envelope, he'd never have to deal with this guy's bullshit again, or anyone else's. Juan took the fateful envelope and turned to walk back to his sleeping area.

He sat down on his bed, slowly. A feeling of intense deja vu began to overwhelm him and pass through his trembling body. He had been in this same position before—once two years ago, and once four years ago... almost to the day. He was shaking. Twice before it had not gone well. He didn't know if he could withstand another parole denial.

He opened the large, turquoise envelope with both reservation and determination. He flipped through the first few pages with cursory care, until he arrived at what mattered. After the departmental jargon, he stopped when he got to the only page in the packet of twenty that meant anything: The Decision of the New York State Board of Parole. This was it. His eyes were conditioned to divert to the one and only line in this entire sea of bureaucratic largesse that meant anything. This time, though, he forced himself to read every line of the portentous executive drivel...but discipline soon gave way to need. His eyes skipped the preliminaries and cut right to the chase...Final Decision: **Parole Denied**. Keep incarcerated for an additional 24 months.

Juan felt his body lose strength, his mind clarity. He wanted to sit down, but realized he was already sitting. He began to fill with anxiety...with worry...with rage! How could this be happening? How could this be happening again, he thought! The agita was now teeming. He threw the papers against his cube wall. He rose from his bed, and began to pace in his confinement.

How could they do this to me again...? He kept asking himself, over, and over again. How could they, after the effort he'd made; the way he'd turned his life around,

gotten his GED, completed multiple vocational certifi-
cations, finished a wealth of voluntary state programs
in an attempt to better himself. How? Why?

What would he tell his family? How could he tell
his family? Another two years in prison and, even after
that, there was no certainty. There was no guarantee.
There was no way of knowing when he'd ever actually
go home. Juan had a life sentence. The maximum time
they could hold him in prison was for his natural life. If
they wanted, they could keep denying his parole every
two years until he slowly, biennially grew older and
older, until one day he died. They might actually keep
him in prison until he died, he thought, among the
throngs who couldn't care less. He would be lost to his
family, his loved ones; another old state number taken
off the facility count, off the statewide count, and carried off into the postmortem correctional abyss. Only
then would he truly be free.

* * *

Juan Martinez was the first of four born to Cristobel and Mercedes Martinez. His parents were young
when they had him, barely out of their teenage years.
They lived in a tiny one-bedroom cottage in the city of
Aguadilla, on the Northwestern shore of Puerto Rico.
Juan's father Cristobel had trouble keeping work, and
good jobs were scarce in Puerto Rico. The family's
poverty worsened with each new sibling, until it was
so bad they decided they had to leave—they had to

move where there was work, steady work. They had to go where there was freedom to pursue a better life, to think and to believe. They had to move to the mainland. They had to move to America.

Mercedes had an older sister who lived in Upstate New York, in the city of Syracuse. She also had a cousin who lived there too. Both had stayed in touch after they had left the island in search of opportunity, in search of something better...and both had found it. They had been trying to persuade Mercedes to move to Syracuse for some time, but the prospect had been frustrated, because of Juan's father. Juan didn't want to leave Puerto Rico either. He was just starting out in his teenage years, he didn't want to leave his family and his friends.

But soon the family's situation could be ignored no further. Things had gotten really, really bad, and they simply had to move and start anew. Soon after Juan's second brother was born, the family took what little they owned and boarded a flight bound for New York, courtesy of a loan from Mercedes's sister and her husband. They were off to start a new life, praying that things would work out. Juan was thirteen. He was scared, and he was worried, but he had no choice.

The Martinez family settled in a small Spanish barrio just west of downtown Syracuse. Hundreds of Puerto Rican families were clustered in the relatively small neighborhood. The neighborhood had its own ethnic markets, park and even its own school. It was like an insular bubble, an oasis in the core of urban diversity—pluralism, rather than multiculturalism. But nobody seemed to object, neither the inhabitants nor the outsiders.

Juan was like any other neighborhood kid; he grew up largely on the streets. Both of his parents worked full-time jobs, and his father also held a part-time job at night. He and his brothers were almost entirely free from adult supervision. They roamed the streets with their group, they played basketball at the park, and they got into selling drugs when school lost its comparative luster. Juan dropped out of high school at sixteen, at the beginning of the tenth grade. His parents objected, but really could do nothing. Neither of them had finished high school either. He started spending more and more time on the corner with the older guys, the more established members of the neighborhood's distinct pecking order. These guys were cool, he thought. They always had the nicest clothes, the flashy bling, the cutest girls and the fastest cars. This was the beginning, and he liked it.

The older guys took Juan in. This was not out of a liking, or a desire to be real friends, but simply out of opportunity. They saw in him another appendage to extend the reach of their growing drug organism, plain and simple. But Juan and others like him never objected. The respect and credibility the new clothes, the jewelry and the flashy car would yield would make any other concern secondary. School was but a distant memory at best now; he saw where his future lay, and he liked it.

As he got better at what he did, the weight of his trade increased. His drug deals grew in value, his possessions grew in worth, and the danger he put himself in rose as well. Juan had just organized the largest transaction of his young career. He had lined up an out-of-town buyer for a large quantity of South American cocaine, Colombian booger sugar. He was to meet this stranger, whom an acquaintance had vouched for, behind the liquor store on Seymour Street on Thursday night. He was to bring the kilo, and with five minutes of work, he'd have the eleven thousand it cost in his pocket. He was set to net three thousand dollars on this one deal alone! Three thousand dollars! The things he could buy with that! In 1983! It was a small fortune to a naive seventeen-year-old just starting out in the game.

Thursday night came sooner than he expected; he'd been waiting for this evening like he used to wait for Christmas. He had procured the product earlier that evening, and he then headed to the liquor store parking lot. He arrived to see a large, black Mercedes sedan idling in the back corner of the tarmac spread. He approached the car. He thought the driver might even need to moor this rig, that's how big it loomed. The windows were heavily tinted, keeping the identity of the car's inhabitants a mystery. As he approached the car, the driver's window lowered slowly. The driver told him to get in the back seat. Juan was a little nervous; this was a huge deal for him. Something felt afoul, but he didn't know what. Stay cool, he thought. Just relax, he kept telling himself, as he felt his heart beat faster and faster. He climbed over the shiny doorjamb, and entered the car. Avarice trumped instinct.

As soon as he closed the door and turned to look at the man sitting next to him, he saw the barrel of a .38 Special come rudely into focus.

"Gimme the fucking blow and you might live, kid," the large Hispanic man said to Juan, as he kept the gun aimed directly at his face.

Holy shit, he thought, how the fuck is this happening? He tried to stay calm. Stay cool. The man in the driver's seat he had glimpsed through the receding tint remained stoic; he kept staring straight ahead, in an unnerving familiarity with this situation. He was the only other person besides the guy with the gun, and himself, in the car. Thoughts raced through his mind...stay calm, but I can't let them rob me of this. I was fronted the $8,000 it costs. How can I go back to my supplier without the money? He'll kill me. I'm through. I have to get out of here with the drugs, he thought.

The man with the pistol demanded the coke again—this time in a much louder, more threatening tone. Juan began to reach slowly into his oversized coat for the package.

"Nice and slow, kid...easy," the man said, as he brought the wrapped brick out of his coat pocket.

He handed it to the man slowly. The man took it, and began to examine the package. He slowly unwrapped the paper covering. The kilo was wrapped well; Juan's attention and the care given were clear.

The man with the gun took his focus off of him just long enough for Juan to see an opportunity.

He seized it, and lunged at the man's arm, forcing the gun upright. It discharged a round through the car's roof. A struggle ensued, the gun flailing in the man's loosening grip, until it fired again. The car was spared this time, but the man holding the gun wasn't as lucky. The bullet had struck him in the jugular. A stream of blood began spurting from his neck as he tried to clutch the wound, helpless and silent now.

The man in the driver's seat by this time had gotten out of the car and was trying to pry Juan from the backseat. He was kicking and punching the driver, anything he could do to get away. He struck the driver in the jaw with a swift kick from his right leg. The man stumbled back a few feet in shock, and Juan jumped at his chance. He leapt from the now-bloodied vehicle, and ran as fast as he ever had from the scene.

Juan was arrested two days later by detectives from the Syracuse Police Department and charged with one count of murder in the second degree. He was remanded to the county jail at his arraignment. No bail. It was over...it was all over. Within just six short months, he would be headed upstate to a maximum-security prison, convicted after trial of the original charge, murder in the second degree. The judge had offered no leniency, despite his lack of a prior criminal record and his adolescence. He sentenced him to the maximum allowable under law: he sent him upstate with a sentence of twenty-five years to life. He was just seventeen. He wouldn't even become eligible for parole consideration until he was forty-two years old, and then he'd only be eligible. All for a drug deal gone horribly wrong.

Juan was devastated and defeated. He still couldn't fully wrap his young mind around what had happened. He kept questioning, and doubting. But he'd been the one getting robbed; he had the gun pulled on him. Wasn't he simply acting in self-defense? Wasn't he trying to escape the situation? It was an accident after all. He never intended to shoot, much less kill, anyone. He had gone to sell a brick of cocaine, not to commit a murder. The courts thought otherwise, and now he had twenty-five years to life to contemplate that night. He had twenty-five long years to ponder how things had turned so violent, so quickly. Juan sat numb on that cramped correctional bus which would cast him off to his new life; a journey which would come to shape and define—to consume and recycle—a directionless soul, as it grew older in the custody of the State.

* * *

Several days had now gone by before Juan was even able to call his family, and let them know of the recent decision. Tell them how he wouldn't be coming home after all. His normal routine began to disintegrate quickly. His friends in the weight pit began to ask where he was. Was he all right? His fellow Christians began to wonder too when he missed Mass three weeks in a row. He never missed church. Ever.

He began to recede into his sleeping area, and withdraw from the masses. He began to separate from life, the only life he'd known for the last twenty-nine years... almost three decades spent in prison. He was now in his late forties. His two children who were born right after he went upstate when he was just seventeen were almost thirty years old now, and his grandchildren were now approaching nine and ten. This all happened while he'd been away...incarcerated.

His depression and despair grew over the months following the parole hearing. He did finally muster the courage to call his children, and tell them he wouldn't in fact be home for the holidays. He had all but promised for those anxious months leading up to the parole board hearing that he'd be home this time. This time would be different, he told them.

How could I have been so weak, so hopeful in the face of this near-certainty? He kept asking himself this. Day-in and day-out, he clawed at a return to his old routine. The regimen that kept him moving forward, that gave him purpose, hope and faith in the face of seemingly unending darkness.

The days became weeks, and the weeks turned into months. The trauma of his third parole denial began to wane, but the abatement was temporary. He found himself sometimes waking in the night, at two, maybe three in the morning. Waking out of an urgency to be conscious...like he felt he was drifting, or falling, through a void of time and space. The feeling was unlike anything he'd ever felt, and it terrified him.

His dreams would turn to horrific nightmares. He would wake in a cold sweat, his pillow damp and his sheets clammy. He'd sit up from the familiar scene, and stare out the window into a land that had become foreign. The glow of the moon would sometimes reflect off the ribbon of razor wire, framing his window to this remote world in an enchantment of lighted lace. This might temper his rising unease, and give him some flicker of hope...some light to strive for at the end of this interminable journey back to life. A light to keep him moving forward, to keep him longing. A light to keep him alive.

Too often though it would do just the opposite. He would begin to think of everything through the prism that is prison. The distortion was often overwhelming, and all hope would evaporate. He was thrust again into the free fall of his life. Juan had no end in sight. He had been free-falling for twenty-nine years from a base jump at seventeen. He had made it this far. His strength and will to survive had triumphed over an attractive resignation, but how much longer could he continue? What's the point anyway? Why does any of it matter anymore? His resolve had petered out. The linchpin of his character was beginning to buckle under the weight of its tow, and this was dangerous.

Juan's life continued to deteriorate. He began to find his way back to his old schedule, his old routine... but it wasn't the same, and everyone noticed. No one seemed able to help. No one seemed able to offer solace and comfort beyond the insincere clichés of prison small talk.

"That's bullshit, Juan! You know how the Parole Board is; it's nothing you did or didn't do, Juan; you've done everything right while in prison; they've gotta let you go sooner or later; I'd put all my money on them letting you go at your next parole hearing; yeah, you're definitely going home then, Juan," they'd say.

He'd heard it all before though. The difference now was, he'd once soaked it up in earnest, but could do so no longer. He used to believe every word, or at least he forced himself to believe every word. It's amazing what the human mind is capable of when cornered. He knew better now, though. Experience is life's best teacher, and he had plenty of that. At least in the area of doing time, which is much harder than most believe. The correctional experience is unlike any other life has to offer, for that exact reason. It is an experience not offered, but rather impressed. It is one in which life as we know it ceases, one where life as mandate becomes norm. Juan was no longer free to live his life as he saw fit; to pursue happiness as he wished. He'd lost that right. Liberty had yielded to justice, and justice had yielded to expediency in the world of corrections.

Over the next year or so, the withdrawal widened. Juan stopped working out entirely. He only rarely attended church, and this was when other members of the congregation practically dragged him to Mass. The resident chaplain was so concerned, he even visited him on several occasions. He personally came to the dorm to speak to him, to offer him support and reassurance from the Lord. The chaplain could sense Juan's faith in God had faded. He assured him it hadn't. The chaplain left unconvinced, but powerless.

Everything that had gone unnoticed up until now was thrust to the fore. The daily things that had once reminded Juan of the freedom he would one day enjoy again, now became crippling. He could no longer read the newspaper, it was simply too disturbing to read of a world he may never see again. Or if he did see it, he didn't know when he'd see it, or if he'd be too old and senile to even appreciate it. The once beloved television, the only real portal to the outside world and the prevailing zeitgeist, became meaningless.

The fellow inmates who were released every morning, those who had reached their prison term's expiration, caused an anger and resentment to boil within him. He felt an overwhelming enmity for his entire life. These prisoners being released once served as fuel for his determination to persevere. They had once fed his hunger to see the door one day too; to free himself from the shackles of his past, and start anew...as a corrected soul, and a repentant Christian.

He longed for this opportunity, for a chance to live a different and better life. He longed to prove to his family, to his government and to the world that he wasn't just a murderer. He was a person, he was a son, he was a father and a brother, and he was a Christian.

But he had committed the highest of high sin, the most punishable of capital crime.

How much time is enough time? Juan wondered this constantly. How much more time can I do? How much more time will change what happened? Will I change anymore than I already have by doing more time? He would grow with resentment, then regret, then sorrow and then despair. Everyone wondered. When are the competing goals of retributive justice and individual rehabilitation satisfied? Can they ever be reconciled? What is the prerogative of a country? What is the duty of a society? What are the responsibilities of individuals? What can be appropriate? What is appropriate? Juan waits for answers to these questions—his life in limbo, his existence in a void. There is no end, no control, no power whatsoever over his destiny...over his fate in this world. He has no power over his life, and this is the price one pays for the taking of another's.

It was a new day though, and the sun shined brightly on the earth. Juan rose quickly this particular morning, put his state clothes on without thinking or hesitation. He laced up his worn state boots. He eyed the strengthening glare of the fluorescent wave, as the light reflected off the shiny institutional floor with each new row coming alight. He'd never trusted places with glossy floors. And then the doubt descended. He wanted to turn back, to curl up in a ball and go to sleep. But he knew he'd awaken in a worse state...and with more laundry to do.

He forces himself through the motions, wills himself to move forward, as he has for twenty-nine years. After all, what choice does he really, honestly have? He thinks of his family. He thinks of his children, his grandchildren. He thinks of his approaching reappearance at the parole board in three months. Even the opportunity to be free at last, gives him hope. He's now been in prison more than three decades. Maybe this will be the one, he thinks. He fills with hope, then fear...then stoic indifference. It's out of his hands, again. But as he stands up slowly from his steel bunk, an ever-so-slight smile pierces the flesh of his hardened face. He turns and walks out of his sleeping area. He heads to morning chow, and to the beginning of another day.

JUST ANOTHER DAY

The sails began to luff with a pleasant cadence. It sounded like a well kept beat on a hand drum. The wind was changing direction. At first it was gradual, then sudden. We needed to commence a port tack now to remain on course. We were headed almost due North toward Luanda, Angola...on the southwestern coast of Africa. We had been following the Skeleton Coast off Namibia for some time, keeping within a mile of the shore so we could enjoy the exotic flora and fauna. This shift in the wind—now a steady northerly gale—would make the next leg of the voyage difficult.

As we turned toward starboard, the boom of the big mono-hulled sloop flew across the deck, nearly taking me with it into the rough sea. We were on a close-hauled tack toward the coast, traveling at a healthy speed. The water sprayed over the bow as we cut through the large swells, sending a brackish mist into my face. It was a clear day. You could feel the power of nature at work. Large birds I could not identify flew overhead. They cut back and forth over the mainsail with uninhibited liberty. We drew closer and closer to the shore, deliberately making a broad zigzag before we tacked back out to sea. I saw several animals in the distance as we approached, a flurry of activity on the cliff that abutted the surging sea.

When we were close enough, I saw that it was a pride of lions tearing apart the carcass of some unlucky prey. There had to be at least eight of them, maybe ten. It was hard to count as they moved so quickly. It was a ravenous frenzy. They clawed and jabbed, moved in and out. They were beautiful, strong and stoic creatures. They moved with a certain confidence and deliberation. It was captivating. These beautiful specimens of God's grandeur were at the top of the food chain, rulers of their kingdom, completely free to roam, pursue and indulge at will. Fascinating.

We were getting awfully close to the shore when I awoke from this fixated stupor. The emerging rocks in the shallow water we found ourselves in were very threatening. We needed to come about and change tack immediately, head back out to sea right then. We prepared to come about. I threw the rudder to my right, and turned the boat furiously into the strong wind ahead. The boat came about, and the boom flew across the deck. I ducked well in advance this time. The sails followed and captured the wind on the leeward side. We were headed back out to sea, away from the lions. We were vulnerable again, as we sailed into the hand of providence…not quite knowing what to expect ahead.

* * *

"COUNT TIME, ON THE COUNT, SITTING OR STANDING," came blaring over the loudspeaker. I was immediately wrenched from my sleep and dragged back down to reality from my dream. I reluctantly rose from my bed, to meet the morose stares of sixty other men. They too were being yanked from their dreams, brought back down to life with jarring haste. My attention was caught by the glisten of the razor wire outside the window, shining with authority in the rising sun. I was still in prison. This was my life. This was the beginning of another day.

The constriction and humility automatically set in, like every other day. With the sun comes the count here. The first of six daily counts taken, as if someone has managed to overcome three fences each topped with a ribbon of razor-wire, motion sensors, cameras and watch towers manned by guards with scoped rifles, and liberal rules of engagement. The count is quickly cleared. Another ordinary day in the total institution of prison has begun.

The deep-seated unease I used to experience in the beginning of my term is no longer present. Yes, it is difficult, to awaken to this day in and day out. But you get used to it. You get used to anything if given enough time. And that's all I have. I got used to it because I had no choice. Either adjust or self-destruct. Not a real tough choice, I thought. This particular day is going to be no different from any other. As you might imagine, life in prison is very different from life on the outside, or more colloquially, life on the "streets" or in the "town." The days are strictly regimented, with no tolerance for deviation. The institution is truly a total institution. The administration is akin to one of a totalitarian regime. The individual here is subordinate to the proper functioning of the whole, that whole being the corrections organism that exists in perpetuity.

The unit is alive. Certainly not flourishing, but alive. Teeth are being brushed, hair is being combed and faces are being shaven. The smell of cheap drip coffee brewing in the hand filter fills the air. CNN's Headline News spends way too long covering Paris Hilton's recent run-in with the law. This time, I understand, it was in Las Vegas. Possession of cocaine. Hardly surprising, yet thirty men stand stuck in awe. Is this really worthy of five minutes of above-the-fold coverage? Must be a slow news day.

Officer Torrent walks through the door, with her usual step and frown on display. The dormitory porters scurry from the woodwork, no attempt at discretion as they clamor for brooms, dustpans and mops. Mr. Rogers is already buffing the recreation room. He has been since six. He's been here for years. Beds are being made, cubes are being cleaned and people are pulling themselves together for another day.

I naturally find myself taking part in the same early-morning routines. In fact, when did routines become a bad thing? That's right, when I came to prison. I look around the dorm to see the mindless execution of an ant farm. I take that back: there is no such coordination and selfless camaraderie. A colony of robots? Possibly. Everyone is concerned with only himself and his immediate needs to survive. The next man means nothing and is of no import. You might wonder why this is; I certainly still do at times. I don't think it was always like this. In fact, now I remember a few old timers at my last facility tell me that it never was like it is today. The penitentiary has changed. There's no unity anymore, no solidarity.

"GET YOUR CUBES STRAIGHT INSIDE-OUT," broadcasts across the dorm loudspeaker.

This is Officer Torrent's signature first command, given each morning at seven-thirty. By this time, however, most cubes are pretty clean. She conducts her first patrol shortly thereafter, cube-standard violation tickets in hand. She'll usually write anywhere from five to ten violations on that first walk through, maybe more if she's having a good day. The inevitable moaning soon follows.

Morning movement finally goes out around eight. There is relative peace on the unit. The commotion and noise of the morning rush retreats, only to return too soon. The inmates with no morning programs remain on the dormitory unit, going about their individual agendas...not those of the State. Chess, dominoes and scrabble are broken out; the tables are arranged close to the TV; the trash talk begins. *You're garbage! I'm gonna wash you up! My niece has more game than you! You clown!* The TV is quickly diverted from the news to music video reruns on MTV. This will be the highlight of the day for many, the outcome of the best of twenty-one games in chess. This treading of water is very unsettling; this "killing time" mentality deeply disturbing.

I made a commitment to myself and to others that I would make the best of this time—this time away from society, my family and friends, my life. I would take the steps I needed to be a better person and live a better life as a result of this experience. Every morning I wake up here, I think of that commitment, that vow I gave at my sentencing hearing before I was ushered off to prison. I have a duty, an obligation. This is not simply doing time for me. I must utilize every passing second of this time to recover and grow as a person, to get to a place where I'm healthy enough and able to help others achieve what I have found.

I usually make my way out to the corner of the recreation room around seven-thirty, right after morning chow. I've jerry-rigged a little office in this corner. I pull two tables into an "L" set-up, sequestered in the corner by one of the pay phones. I set my typewriter on one table, and lay out whatever I'm working on top of the other. I have my steaming cup of Folgers instant coffee in hand. I sit down and get to work. Reverse. I read The Wall Street Journal for an hour, then get to work. Here I sit from around seven-thirty in the morning until two in the afternoon, with a break for lunch at eleven-thirty. I get the most work done in this little nook, despite the surrounding confusion.

The tables sit back to the side of the recreation room, which is probably roughly eight hundred square feet. The TV is constantly on, and not simply on. It is turned up to usually the loudest it will go. This I still don't understand, as the people watching are within ten feet. Despite the loud TV, the banter and the overall disquietude of the area, I've actually gotten fairly good at tuning out the cacophony. Again, you get used to anything, and I don't have a choice, if I want to get anything done in here.

When people think of prison, and doing time, they usually imagine a bunch of downtrodden inmates sitting around in cells doing nothing. Sure, that happens, but more so in the maximum-security prisons, with longer sentences and much less hope in the air. In contemporary prison, inmates are required to participate in programs, whether it's for an assessed need for academic, vocational or substance abuse therapy. Often times it is all three. The day is strictly apportioned around these programs, recreation, meals, and other extracurricular activities. It is very easy for the inmates to "fake it to make it;" to do the bare minimum to satisfy the "assessed need" imposed by the State. The tragedy lies in the fact that this is the modus operandi of the majority.

I head back to my cube maybe mid-morning for a five minute respite…maybe get another cup of mud, maybe just make a cursory glance at my area, just make sure things are in order. I find a yellow carbon copy of a cube standard violation on the top of my big locker. You gotta be kidding me, I think. The care and attention I take to avoid this very thing...come on! *Locker needs to be centered in cube between bed and partition,* it read in barely legible scratch. My small locker had been ever so slightly askew, just off center, as I had been rummaging earlier and must have moved it slightly from its home.

Annoyed, I crumple up the violation—making sure Officer Torrent doesn't witness my disdain—and walk back out to my "office." Here I might spend the remainder of the morning, doing whatever it is I might be doing that particular day. If I've captured the elusive muse, and feel particularly creative, I'll work on my short stories. If I need to write an essay or response for a course, I'll open the syllabus. I may just read whichever book I am currently reading. Or I might catch-up on my correspondence with various family and friends. Maybe it's crossword time. Maybe I'll just sit and think, stare at the institutional cinder block, and contemplate. Muse. Ponder. Whatever it may be, I feel most comfortable in the "office."

I cannot even call it my "office." It is not mine. Nothing is mine in here, really. This is not home, this is merely where I live, for now. This is where I've been placed for what I have done. I have to accept the things I cannot change, but also I must find the courage and resolve to change the things I can. This is why I spend my time the way I do. This is how I remember to live my life each and every day I awake to sixty other mugs and the glare of razor wire lacing the landscape just outside my window. This is one of the few choices I CAN make, on my own, without the State offering "guidance," or telling me directly what to do and how to do it.

Two o'clock rolls around faster than I realize. It's ten of, and I have to get ready to go workout. I tidy-up the "office," and hurry to my cube to change. I notice some of my neighbors doing the same thing. Afternoon program run has just gone out a little while ago; the dorm is relatively "quiet," quotation marks emphasized. It is never quiet here. Ever. Even in the middle of the night, there are at least four or five Bunyans chopping down sequoias.

That is literally what it sounds like, no embellishment. Had I not procured a set of earplugs on the black market from a guy I know on the lawns and grounds gang, I'd be denied the only real escapism and peace in here: a dream state. A place where you're undisturbed for six short hours, from the last count of one day, until the first count of the next. This is the only true egress from this world, as temporary and artificial as it is.

I may get pulled over en route to the yard for my workout, or I may not. It's a random search. "Random," so they say. If it's so random, why is it always the same people getting pulled over and frisked? It's always young to middle-aged, muscular, slightly intimidating black men. This is who is up against the wall,

legs spread, face pressed against the sandpaper brick...
getting their persons violated, their selves humiliated.
This is in front of the hundreds of others strolling right
past, without a hitch, ever. Most of these men walking
by are white.

Is this not racial profiling? Of course this is racial
profiling. This is where racial profiling began. This is
the mecca, the birthplace. This is a facility with over
two hundred and fifty employees—security and civilian staff. Out of this staff, I think I've seen one person
of a minority background. He was a middle-aged black
officer, male, who gave the noticeable impression
he hated his job and where he was. On the flip side,
the inmate population is overwhelmingly of minority make-up. Close to three-quarters of the general
inmate population is African-American or Hispanic.
These two minorities account for just over a third of
the country's general population. The overrepresen-
tation in prison is stunning. This is a huge problem.
Is anyone ever going to do anything about this? What
can be done about this? Why does this continue to be
ignored?

I come back from my two-hour workout at the four
o'clock return, the last inmate movement before the
4:30 p.m. count. Officer Ransom is back from his two-
day break...fuck. He's also more commonly referred
to on the unit as Ram-Rod, The Raminator, or just
simply douche bag. He's not too popular among the
inmates, as you might have guessed from his endear-
ing nicknames. This is because this guy's strictly by the

book. Strictly. I mean this guy is a walking manual on Department of Corrections protocol. Seriously. When he writes tickets, which is on the regular, he doesn't even consult the rulebook, like every other officer. He doesn't need to, he has it memorized. Disobeying a direct order? Tier II, 106.10. Out of place? Tier II, 102.30. Disrespecting an officer? Yeah hold on, let's call the sergeant. Probably going to be a 112.10, and you'll have thirty days in solitary confinement to mull over whether it was worth actually calling him a douche bag to his face.

He'll tell me I'm on the dormitory cleanup, as if I somehow forgot what my job has been for the past ten months. I'll tell him I know. I make my protein shake, wash-up quick after my workout and grab my porter weapons. I'm going to tackle the dorm. It's the same routine, every day: Sweep, mop and dust the sills in the dorm area. I get the same stupid comments from fellow inmates as I sweep past their cubes. *Good job. Ram-Rod must be back. Nice technique.* Assholes.

Then I might encounter the stray comedian, who thinks it's funny to throw trash into the aisle just before I pass with the broom. That's cool, thanks for that. I try to get this done as quickly as I can. After all, I'm getting paid seventeen cents an hour. No, that's not a typo. Seventeen cents. So I give the state what they pay me for, as required. Nothing more, nothing less. Sometimes when Officer Ransom is absent, I'll even subcontract my job out. There is an oversupply of willing independent contractors in prison, plus I place a rather high opportunity cost on my time. If I can give someone a cup of coffee so I can remain in the "office" writing—undisturbed by the menial calling of the State—I will. In a heartbeat. Every time.

"ATTENTION IN THE COMPOUND: SOFTBALL GAME IN THE YARD TONIGHT, FOLLOWED BY THE BASKETBALL CHAMPIONSHIP BETWEEN "F" DORM AND "A" DORM. RELEASE YOUR ONE AND TWO SIDES OUT TO RECREATION."

I wish they would turn the loudspeaker down…it's way too loud. The dorm depletes from its usual raucous state. From sixty to ten, just like that. I love when evening recreation goes out. I head straight back to the "office." It's time to take advantage of the next couple of hours while it's actually quiet. I'll finish where I left off in the "office" at two.

"ATTENTION IN THE COMPOUND: OPEN YOUR DOORS FOR THE RECREATION EXCHANGE!"

I had lost track of time, immersed in my writing or reading, or whatever it was I was doing. I quickly grab anything of value, and rush back to my cube. I throw it all in my locker, change quickly, grab my book and a quick cup of mud with the hot-pot water. I lock my locker and dash out the door just as they announced it: "SECURE YOUR DOORS. RECREATION RUN IS COMPLETE."

I cut it close again. I'm going to work after all. If I'm a little late, don't they have to let me out anyway? Won't the facility come to a screeching halt without my presence in the recreation equipment shack? Probably not. But then who'd take the IDs and hand out the lifting belts? The basketballs? The horseshoes? The paddles? I have to think they'd manage.

I get pulled over at the gate to the yard. It's Officer Smitty. He must be back from his vacation. Smitty is one of the most racist officers in this compound. But it's not overt, on-the-sleeve racism. If you're white, you're good with him...never a problem. He'll pull you aside and talk with you, almost like you're not a convict. If he likes you even a bit, then you'll see the racism in all its true colors. And it's grotesque.

"You decided to show up for work, huh?" he says with a slight grin, intimating he might have unearthed my recent gambit.

While Smitty was on vacation, I too was on vacation. For the past week-and-a-half, I have been paying someone a stamp (forty-four cents) to go sit out in the recreation equipment shack for my shift, from eight-thirty until ten at night. The state pays me fifty-one cents for the same shift, so it makes sense (and cents! a robust profit of seven-cents a shift!). More importantly, and the real reason I outsourced my presence, I can stay in the "office" uninterrupted for the entire three-and-a-half hours of evening recreation time, when the vast majority of the dorm is outside. It is somewhat quiet in the dorm then. Halcyon, almost. Almost.

"What do you mean, Smitty? I've been here," I proffer in reply.

"My ass you have. Don't lie to me; I have eyes and ears everywhere in this place," he said, as his smile turned to a frown.

I knew I was caught. I'd better just stop digging, just tell him the truth. He obviously knew. The guy did have informants all over the compound. Fuck. I should have known better. I knew that too. Fuck.

"Okay, here's what happened. I had an arrangement with a friend who said he'd cover the equipment shack for me for the last week or so. I've been really busy with a whole..."

He put up his hand.

"Shhhh...I don't give a fuck, Weimer. I don't wanna hear your little story. In fact, I don't really give a shit who mans that dumbass shack anyhow, as long as someone is in there. Just let me know next time you want to do something like that, and don't make a habit out of it," he said, his frown turning to an ever-so-slight grin.

He motioned me back into the stream of inmates funneling into the tiny gate to the yard. I said no more, made my way into the current, and disappeared.

It's the same thing every night: hand out a few belts, a few balls, maybe a paddle. Then I usually just sit in the shack, or outside on the pail if it's nice, and read. Sometimes I read my current book, sometimes the paper I may not have finished, maybe do a crossword. It's only an hour-and-a-half. I talk to a few acquaintances, maybe even do a loop around the yard if the cop's cool. Then it's over. My shift, and the day. I think about the day, the week, the year...my life. The stars are bright, the air crisp. The season has definitely changed.

I think of my family, my parents, my brother. This fills me with love and hope, every time. I think of my friends, the support they provide too. I think of how fortunate I am to have all of this in my life; so many in here have neither. So many have grown up in a world alone, forced to fend for themselves and survive any way they can. This makes me sad. I must persevere though. I must be strong. I must continue learning, healing, growing. I must continue helping those I can, those who want it. I'm okay. Life is okay.

I close the equipment shack up, and gather my stuff to head back to the dorm for the count and the night. Everyone in the yard makes their way out of the recreation area, and heads back to their dorms for the nightly lock-in. As I slowly walk back to my building, a fellow inmate from my dorm passes me.

"Another day down, Weimer...another day down," he says to me, as he continues on.

"Yeah...one day closer to home," I reply, as a smile comes across my cold face.

VICIOUS CIRCLE

The sky was clear and the air dry. Cold and snowy, that December had been. The flurries had been intermittent the last few days. Like every other Tuesday evening at seven-thirty, the meeting was called over the facility's loudspeaker. And on every Tuesday, it felt like deliberate defiance. The largely lone members would sift through the recreation room recess, and finally make it to the dormitory door. They would gladly exit the chaos, and enter the bitter peace of the night. They were headed to a brief but everlasting hour of recovery.

They merged on the walkways, in pursuit of the same destination, the same goal. The long faces and flat eyes changed to open faces and eyes wide. Smiles emerged and niceties were exchanged. The initial joy was always tempered at the door, when reality was re-administered by the doorman jailer. But this was only temporary, the collective will too strong to be deterred.

The members of the fellowship filed in, one after another. Hands were shaken and greetings traded.

The layers unfurled and the line at the coffeepot grew. The aroma was bold and inviting. The members settled and the meeting began. The ensuing routine was the only such routine welcomed in this dark place called prison, a place where routines had become loathed. It was a routine to be seized and looked forward to. It was a routine aimed not at control, but rather guidance. It was a routine driven by attraction, not subjugation.

The chairman went through the formalities, and then opened the floor to discussion. Hands soon shot up, as they always did. This was one of the very few places in prison where talking and sharing were valued; where honesty and vulnerability became assets in an otherwise illiquid market. Jackets could be comfortably unfolded, and emotions released without the expected judgment. The usual democracy of the group had yielded this particular evening, not to caprice, but to intention. The hands held high were momentarily put down, at the creative direction of the chairman, he who was charged with the facilitation of the group that evening.

"Round-Robin it will be tonight," he exclaimed.

"After you share, you select who shares next."

This was a surprise, but one not derided it. While certainly not de rigueur, it was soon embraced by almost all in the group. Change can be good. He called on Michael after he was finished speaking. He startled him, and caught him unprepared. He'd been sitting in the corner by the door, in an unassuming manner. He was almost visibly reserving the right to get up and leave if he had to, for whatever reason he might furnish.

You could tell he was annoyed. He was annoyed by this fellow directing the meeting, who'd prompted him to come to life and be present. He sent a deep, piercing look at him, then refocused his steady stare on the indistinct cinder block on the opposite side of the room, quietly mulling the decision to share or buck the challenge. He'd already shown up to the meeting three times now. Wasn't that enough? Why'd he have to talk? Why did he have to share? Those five seconds he spent contemplating felt like five minutes.

The room waited in anticipation, eager to hear from this mysterious newcomer. And then he spoke, as silence was trumped. He introduced himself cautiously, exactly identifying what he considered important. He spoke with the care of a politician. He was nervous and anxious, like everyone is at first. This place is foreign to the prison yard populace, much like prison is to the general populace. He spoke slowly and carefully, and everyone listened intently.

He spoke of how he landed in prison, how he landed in an otherwise barren room surrounded by the furniture of the fellowship and not much more. It was part mandate, part admission. He was desperate at this point, and desperation had been generous with Michael. He spoke of how this was his sixth state prison term. He spoke of how he'd been in and out of prison for the last twenty-five years, since he was twenty years old. The math alone was arresting. He'd lost everything: his family, his wife, his daughter who now refused to speak to him. Everything. Michael described an addiction nothing short of stunning, an addiction that had swept up and consumed anything that ever meant anything to him in satisfaction of its unending hunger. It was an appetite so ravenous it was incapable of negotiation. It truly was as they said: crack cocaine was the Devil's bait.

Michael went on to detail his life's story, how it'd moved him further and further from everything he loved and valued. For what, though? He didn't know, and no one else knew either. He only knew the pain and loss cocaine always caused was only numbed by more, and that more was always never enough. It was never, ever enough. His punishments were never, ever enough for him to learn. They were never enough to force him to change what he couldn't change on his own, for reasons he knew not.

The room sat fixed on this man, this stranger pouring out his heart and soul to other strangers, in the strangest of environments. Everyone in that room could relate. Everyone could relate to a degree, but to a degree, nonetheless. And that was the point. He shared and spilled and admitted and bemoaned, and it was halting. Foreheads wrinkled and eyebrows ascended. The empathy was so heavy it was almost suffocating.

Michael had come to the meeting for whatever reason, and was now sharing for whatever reason. He was sharing though, and that was what was important.

He went on and on; it seemed natural and in need of release. He poured out years of buried emotion, and the stiff facade of prison began to crumble in that small room. He talked and they listened, and then it was over. And the overwhelming silence returned.

* * *

It was springtime when Michael went home after that last state prison term. April it was, when that fifth prison sentence had finally expired and deposited him back into society. He'd been untethered from the tight grip of prison, and thrust to the lesser leash of parole. The colors of life were in full bloom when he got out. The contrast from just days prior was stark to the observant eye, to the careful spectator who knew and respected the power of those things beyond his control. These things went unnoticed by Michael though. He had other things on his mind, more important concerns than the power of rebirth reflected in his surroundings. Michael had plans and ideas; things were going to be different this time. Things had to be different this time.

Michael found a job within a week, which surprised his parole officer. Hell, it even surprised him a little. He landed a gig at Syracuse Banana, a fresh produce distributor on the North Side of Syracuse off Butternut Street. He had simply gone in after seeing a job ad. I might as well try, he thought. Gotta start somewhere. He had brought with him no resume, just a clean shave and a prayer. He got into a conversation with the hiring manager for what seemed like over an hour. Sports, mutual friends and his record were what they discussed. After their exchange, the guy on the other side of the desk extended an offer to Pat, right there, to begin as soon as he could.

Things then began to come together. Michael landed the job as a truck loader, was living rent-free at the Rescue Mission, and his parole officer seemed to be all right, at least compared to his past parole officers. He went to the mall right after he received his first paycheck two weeks later. He had almost four hundred dollars, after having paid back his boss the initial advance he'd given him on day one. He needed new clothes badly. He only had two outfits, and one was his state release clothes, which were no longer a wardrobe option.

He bought new Wolverine work boots with steel-toed tips and a supportive steel shank. He bought a few pairs of jeans, his whites, a sweatshirt, shirt, and a cheap watch for twenty dollars. He only had forty dollars left. Then it struck. Out of an otherwise clear mind it appeared, and out of hibernation its cunning grip returned: forty dollars would be enough for a great afternoon ride on the Crack High Express, he thought to himself. NO! Not this time! I promised myself and my family. NO, I can't do this again! I know where it takes me…every time: prison!

His resolve to strive for something better, and the temporary distraction of cinnamon rolls baking in the distance, won out this time. Michael continued walking toward the food court and bought a meatball sub at Subway, and a fresh-out-of-the-oven cinnamon roll from Cinnabun. He enjoyed both more than they deserve to be enjoyed, and then it dawned on him: he only had thirty-two dollars left out of his paycheck, a paycheck which needed to last him two more weeks until the next paycheck! He was so used to the all-expenses-paid lifestyle perk of his vacation in state prison, courtesy of the "Always Vacancy" hospitality of New York State's Department of Corrections, that he'd forgotten how to plan. He'd forgotten how to budget, how to manage his own affairs and money.

As he made his way back to the Rescue Mission on the Centro bus line, the anxiety retreated. He knew he didn't have rent to worry about living at the Rescue Mission, he could grab meals at the shelter, if he absolutely had to, and now he had all the clothes he needed. I'll be alright, he thought. At least I'm not still in prison. Anything's better than that.

The following days passed without incident or event. They slowly turned into weeks, until he realized he'd now been out and free for exactly five weeks. And he was still clean! He grew proud, and his resolve to persevere clean and sober hardened. He knew this time would be different. He refused to do what he'd done every time before, which was use and wind up back in prison. No, not doing that this time.

It was a Tuesday afternoon when his boss called Michael into his office. He told him to sit down; he had some bad news. Michael grew weary and began to shake, and his boss told him. He had just received a call from Michael's sister...their mother had just died. Michael was shocked...but relieved, in a way. He thought he was losing his job, or his parole officer had called with some allegation. Michael was unfortunately still the first thing on Michael's mind. It's not to say he didn't love his mother, and wish she hadn't died, but they'd grown apart over the years. Over the two-plus decades he'd been back and forth from the pen to the streets, their relationship had continued to deteriorate. He paid her a visit on the second day he was free this time, but hadn't seen her since. And now she was gone—forever.

The funeral was held that following Monday evening, at Francone & Sons on the near Westside. Michael had borrowed a suit from a friend at work. It didn't fit him very well, but he had no choice. He didn't really care how it looked anyhow. He grew nervous and his steps felt heavy as he approached the funeral home. He knew all his family would be there: his siblings, his ex-wife, his daughter. His daughter was now fifteen, and he hadn't seen her in over five years. He probably wouldn't even recognize her now, he thought. He'd been writing to her three, maybe four times a year for the last couple of years he had been locked up. But he never received a response, never got so much as a reply or an acknowledgement. This might be the time though; it might be different now, he thought. He was home and he could start anew, forget the past and move on. Yes, this was his start, he thought.

Michael stood alone and in the back of the funeral hall, so it would be harder for people to stare. They'd have to turn around, and that was too rude at a funeral. But he was wrong. They turned and they stared, almost everyone in the parlor, except for his daughter, who looked like she'd grown a foot since he saw her last. Michael felt like he was on stage at some carnival sideshow. The humiliation and shame was overwhelming—almost so great that he might have left, had it not been for his daughter. Ashley was keeping him there; she was all he cared about now. Not his brothers, not his sisters, not his ex-wife, not his old friends. Only her. And this was his chance to start a new relationship with her. As soon as the service was over, he'd approach her. Perfect, he thought.

As the ceremony came to a close, he moved closer to the front of the room, where Ashley was standing with her mother, Jennifer. Jennifer was Michael's third and most recent ex-wife. On his way over to his daughter, he was forced to speak to his siblings, a few friends of the family and some distant relatives. But only out of respect for his mother did he do this. Where the hell were they for his last prison term? Or what about the four before that? No letters but maybe one? No answer to pleas for a little money? Just ten dollars, maybe? They didn't even come visit me, when I was an hour away! Fuck 'em...I don't need them anyway! Some family they'd been.

And then he saw her face emerge from the crowd gathered by the lectern. As if he could see no other,

Ashley's was there, shining in the soft orange light of the otherwise dark room. He approached his ex-wife first...then quickly reconsidered. He didn't want to ruin the opportunity if they started to argue. He shifted his focus again upon Ashley, and had walked almost right up to her before she finally saw him. He made eye contact, and that was all it took.

Ashley's face receded from sorrow to dread almost instantly. She instinctively turned, and moved away at a pace just shy of inappropriate. Michael was frozen in place. He felt as heavy and immobile as a rock. He was stuck. Jennifer noticed her daughter's departure. She turned around to find the source of her unease, and was taken with similar disgust. She gave Michael a long, reducing stare...a stare for which he had no response, no expression but the obvious emptiness shown on his vacant face. She too turned, and followed her daughter's lead out of the large, dimly lit room. And that was it. Michael's only real chance at beginning to salvage any relationship he may have once had with his only daughter was now gone...lost, another failure to add to the lengthy list of his life.

The pain he felt grew with force. He turned and left the funeral home. He was furious, sad and devastated at once. He ignored the entreaties as he hurried out of the building. All that he valued—the only thing he even cared about anymore—was now reduced to nothing. His relationship with his daughter was basically nonexistent, and may forever be that way for all he knew. The pain surged like a torrent, but this time it was going to be different. He kept repeating this in his clouded mind. This time it's going to be different.

But it wasn't different, and maybe it could never be different. The pain was just too much; what there was left to live for too little. He headed straight to the place that had always given him relief. Temporary relief, but relief. He needed it. Just this once, right now. It's just too much to bear...all of it. His life, his loss...everything! The pain was simply too much for him to bear. After I calm my nerves and get high, I'll work out a plan to win Ashley back, he thought. Tomorrow I'll do that. Right now though, he headed for relief. He went straight to the crack house he'd known for over a decade.

He only had twenty dollars on him, but that's all he needed, he knew. It was just enough to get him high for a couple of hours and obscure the pain. And that's all he needed, he kept repeating. But it was never all he needed. Somewhere deep down in the recesses of his soul, he knew before he smoked that first hit, that it wasn't all he needed. But the urge was simply too strong to be overcome by reason or history. Michael bought the drugs, and he smoked the crack. He instantly felt relieved, and he felt guilty—but he felt removed. Removed from the situation...from his life...from reality.

And then it happened: his care and concern shifted entirely from reality, to doing anything and everything in his power to keep reality from resettling. For Michael, this meant only one thing, as it always did: staying high for as long as humanly possible. Putting off the misery of his life for as long as he could. The high began to wear off, and so did his resolve to make this time the one that was different. He was out of money, but his hunger for the crack high was still on its first course. He left the crack house, and the spree commenced.

Over the next five days straight, Michael slept not one wink. He was suspended somehow between life and unconsciousness by the steady administration of cocaine into his withering body. He was losing two, maybe three pounds a day. He was stealing anything not bolted down across three counties to sustain and finance his unrelenting crack high. Burglaries, larcenies and a few robberies were now the norm for him, each day bringing a new host of crime and destruction to pay the dealers and feed the hunger. His eyes steadily grew more and more wide, yet his reception fell with equal vigor. He was turning into a monster, a walking zombie, a frail representative of human will run riot. And who knew when it would have ended, when he would have succumbed to cardiac arrest, if it weren't for the intervention. The intervention came by way of the law, by reality, by forced abstinence.

On the sixth morning of this epic bender, Michael was arrested by a platoon of State Troopers and Syracuse Police Officers as he walked along what he thought was a safe side street on the South Side of Syracuse. Two vans pulled up without warning, screeched to a halt as the doors slid to allow the will of no less than twelve officers to unfold. Michael turned and ran immediately upon seeing and hearing the vans. The cops gave chase, and it was all over in a matter of moments. He didn't make it twenty yards.

He was tightly cuffed and taken to the State Police barracks. Here he was thrust into a stadium-lit interrogation room, already inhabited by three detectives. He was told how he was being charged with an incomparable string of crimes. Dozens and dozens of charges were read to him as he sat, eyes falling flat, in the corner on the old steel chair. He was told how he was also suspected in several other incidences, and how they were currently being investigated by a host of law enforcement agencies working in conjunction. More charges would surely follow, he was told. But the words being told him weren't heard. He listened, because he had to, but he didn't hear what they were saying. Nothing registered. He hadn't slept in over one hundred and twenty hours; nothing could register at that point, even if he wanted it to.

He was fingerprinted, photographed and led away to an awaiting police cruiser. He was taken to the county jail, where he'd await further charges and court proceedings. Here he'd await arraignment on those further charges, and eventually trial on the whole battery of allegations. Michael didn't comprehend what was happening. Not yet, at least. He sat in that cell for what felt like two more days, awake, but not present. The cocaine was still pulsating its powerful pollution through his weakened veins. He stood up pacing, then sat down still. He couldn't sleep. He would kill to sleep right now, but he couldn't. Michael wanted to fall asleep forever. He was afraid he'd never wake. Would that be better, he thought? He was torn. He was weak and afraid, and now he was right back in a cell again… with no one but himself.

In the coming weeks Michael would be arraigned on multiple charges: burglary, grand larceny, trespassing, robbery, breaking & entering, possession of drugs…the list went on and on. Multiple counts on some, denied bail on all by a furious judge who'd already sentenced Michael to prison twice before in just the past decade. The allegations trickled in as he began to slowly recover from a bender that drained him of everything but a pulse. Again. Additional law enforcement agencies would catch the strong scent of Michael's destructive modus operandi, and add to the insurmountable dossier. In all, he faced twenty-four felony charges spanning three counties, nine townships, and in the jurisdiction of several competing agencies.

Over the coming months as his weighty indictment made its slow way through the legal rigmarole of pretrial proceedings, Michael would eventually plead guilty to a slew of charges. Others were dropped in satisfaction of his admission of guilt to the most serious. All of this came at the urging of an overworked and underpaid public defender. Guilty by jury conviction after trial was all but certain. He couldn't take the risk of losing at trial and facing the maximum sentences. The state's cases against him were almost impenetrable. The evidence was simply overwhelming: fingerprints, DNA, witness testimony, every prosecutorial piece of ammunition save a confession. The judge had already warned he'd impose the maximum penalties on Michael for any charges he was found guilty of after trial, if he chose to waste the time and money of the court and the taxpayers to prove what the judge said he already knew: Michael's guilt.

The eventual plea deal he agreed to satisfied the whole swarm of charges in the multiple criminal complaints pending against him. The judge ran some sentences wild (consecutive) and some together (concurrent). As Michael stood there blank faced that day at sentencing, he finally was able to comprehend what was happening. The time imposed began to stack-up like Lincoln Logs. One state prison term on top of another, rested still on yet another, to be followed by more still. His consciousness grew with every new term uttered by the distant man cloaked in black. He didn't know if he was going to be able to overcome this mountain of time with any health or sanity. And this was Michael, who knew how to hold and do time better than a timepiece.

It had now been one hundred and seventy-four days since his arrest, and he hadn't woken up until now. Michael was ultimately sentenced to a hodgepodge of separate state terms in prison. Each alone might have been easier to comprehend, maybe even to accept, but not together…not taken in their looming aggregate. Not this time, the sixth time. Michael was sent upstate on the correctional bus to nowhere facing down 9-27 years in prison. He wouldn't even be eligible for release consideration until he was fifty-four, when his daughter was twenty-four. And more likely than not he'd be locked up until his late sixties, if he even lasted that long. His daughter would be in her mid-thirties, far past the point of forgiveness for her father's countless failures. She'd be too deep into her own life by then, and too hurt and too hardened by his years of destruction.

This is what Michael thought of in his new consciousness. He didn't think of how he'd manage 9-27 years in prison so much, but rather how he'd just thrown away any chance of being in his daughter's life again. He sat on the bus, shackled to other state prison commitments headed north, and this is all he could think of. He stared without purpose or interest at the people on the streets as they passed—people who were always distant, but who now seemed foreign. Their liberty or happiness didn't bother Michael. He'd been through this before, he'd been hardened long ago. What bothered him was what he had done to his daughter—again.

* * *

The novelty of this new prison Michael found himself in after his transfer had been lost to the very sameness from which it once stood apart. So had the intrigue of a new dorm, and the challenge of a new job. The expected and the mundane had indeed returned to govern his life, just like they always seemed to, after even the shortest lull. He had only been there for three months, and this is where he now called home: Cayuga Correctional Facility.

It was his sixth facility in four years. Just when he'd gotten comfortable, established a few hustles, was finally able to eke out a living...Bam!

"Pack your shit, you're on the transfer draft shipping out tomorrow," the State would say to him.

It seemed to never fail. He'd gotten used to this in a way, and yet he hadn't. He'd sold hope and expectation to resignation and submission long ago. Those luxuries weren't even accessible anymore. Not to Michael, at least.

Every day was identical. They'd merge into weeks, blend into months, and then coalesce into years. But this never happened fast enough; it was never fast enough. It was as if you were suspended in time, hung out to dry outside the steady revolution of the world. Then, upon expiration, slung back into the foreign orbit of life, now expected to succeed among unfamiliar and better-trained peers in society.

Michael was up at five every morning, even on weekends. He got up to clean the dorm, to stay busy and active, detached from the reality of his situation the only way he now knew how. He'd brew that first cup of coffee in a series of what might easily exceed ten by day's end. He did this to jumpstart his tired body and pry the flat eyes open to at least half-mast. He'd go sweep the porch and have his first of many, many cigarettes—loose Bugler tobacco rolled hastily between three fingers of one hand. He'd become a master roller over the years.

By six Michael had already done more than most had by noon. At six he was off to work for his six-hour shift in the Mess Hall as a kitchen worker. He earned Grade-Four pay, which is why he took the position, and why he was living comfortably now. This enabled him to go shop every two weeks at the commissary with eighteen dollars instead of his usual seven. He got his three bags of coffee, six pouches of tobacco, a couple bars of Dial soap and called it a buy.

He'd be out of work by noon before he knew it, back on the dormitory unit getting ready for the yard. He'd usually then go out at one and work out to relieve some tension and stay in shape. Then he might walk around after, bullshit with the boys a bit, which he always did, no matter the weather or the mood he was in. The negativity and retrospect of the yard was simply too attractive for most to resist.

The prison recreation yard offered a unique perspective into a past ungoverned by the mores of life or the rule of law. It was a time and a place to briefly forget the looming reality of the situation: prison. It was a place where war stories were shared and met with broad acceptance; where sexual conquests were detailed and reminisced; where partying achievements were listed off like life accomplishments.

Michael was no different from the moving majority of the main yard mass. He told stories, spoke of his countless paid-for-pussy extravaganzas and, most disturbingly, spoke of those crack highs—those binges which routinely placed him in the very position to lament, not exult, his life. He was well liked in the yard. He had throngs of friends and was cool with all the major cliques. But this was for all the wrong reasons.

He'd walk back to the dorm after these sessions feeling drained, defeated and cheated. Inside, he was all of these, and more. Inside, he was slowly rotting away; the detritus that had become his life now finally coming into sharp focus. This was his sixth state prison term! Six! How the fuck did this happen? How did this happen, again! He'd ask himself this over and over, but never lend enough attention to the cause which lay so plainly in front of him...seen by all but the polluted eye of an addict.

His family had written him off long ago. They had disowned him after he landed his third state prison bid. His friends had left earlier still, if you'd even call them friends. And now his only child, his daughter Ashley, wouldn't even talk to him. She couldn't stand to look him in the face for so much as an instant. Michael had lost everything, because of one thing. And somehow, in spite of all this, he wanted more than anything to get high.

Michael was peculiar among addicts. Of all his time spent in prison over the decades, he'd never once gotten high in prison. Not on pot, not on hooch, not on heroin, not on cocaine. Nothing, ever, in prison. All of these were available in bounty behind the prison fences. But his abstinence in prison was not out of a desire to change or to recover. He knew the quantity and quality of the drugs in prison simply wouldn't be enough for him. His problem was not in prison, but rather when he hit the streets. He couldn't manage his addiction, and he couldn't manage his life. He couldn't manage anything but his time in prison, which he unfortunately did with unusual deftness. It's freedom that's his problem. It's the world that's his problem. It's his self that's his problem.

Not long after Michael arrived at this new but ordinary facility, he was presented with an opportunity to change. He was given a real chance to address his problem and his addiction, but he refused the offered rehabilitation program. He told the corrections counselor how he still had four more years until his first parole board. This was his minimum board review date, which he'd probably be denied anyhow.

It was way too early to take something like that now, he told the counselor. He'd do it later, closer to his parole board hearing. His counselor tried to sway him to reason—to honesty—but it was hopeless. With someone as implacable and incapable of self-reflection as Michael, change is almost impossible. But his counselor persisted.

She spoke to Michael of an international program that had worked for thousands of troubled souls, and had helped those who'd struggled their whole lives with demons they simply could not conquer on their own. She spoke of a fellowship, a group and a consciousness larger than oneself. She spoke of the role of a Higher Power to help guide those afflicted back to sanity. She told him how it helped lead them back to the path of life, to the path of freedom and personal liberty.

At first Michael resisted this too, but she again persisted. She saw the tragedy reflected in his eyes, and confirmed by his thick record folder that lay in front of her. She felt compelled to spend the extra effort. This looked like his last chance. This really was his last stop before the train of addiction deposited him at death or insanity. She suggested and explained, and he sat there listening. His eyes were flat, but engaged. He wasn't just listening to her, he was actually hearing what she was saying.

Michael knew deep down this had to end. He couldn't keep living like this. He'd become an animal, one domesticated and more comfortable in his prison cage than in the wild. He'd become institutionalized. He was finally scared by his reality, by his staggering losses and his bleak future should he continue to rely on his own self-will. He desperately needed to stop trying to direct the play of his life, and start to simply act in it. She spoke and he heard her. He related to what she said. He even saw some hope on the horizon.

The following week Michael saw his name on the Call-Out sheet, just as she said it would appear should he consent to join the group. He had agreed to go, and he felt immediately uneasy upon seeing his name on the sheet, but yet he also felt a bit comforted. He was comforted by the promise and by the prospect. Maybe things could be different. Maybe he wasn't destined to die in prison or in some back alley...alone, broke and devoid of life. He still didn't know when he'd ever get back out on the streets, or even what he'd do when he did finally make it out, but maybe he didn't need to know now.

Maybe just the hope of something better, of something different than what he'd come to expect of himself and of life...maybe that was enough. Maybe this would finally be enough. Maybe he could arrive at *enough* and be content, if just for today. This brought the slightest of smiles to his face, and that was enough. He turned and rushed back to his cube area to get his coat and hat before they called the facility movement to the evening group meeting...the meeting that just might save his life.

SWALLOWED PRIZE

There was nothing extraordinary about this particular morning. The same things were going on, the same routines were being followed, the same conversations carried. Gee was brewing another cup of joe by the microwave. This was probably his third cup of coffee today, and it wasn't even noon yet. He strained every last drop of the dark Bustelo through the filter he had fashioned with a plastic clothes hanger and a handkerchief. The clear water from his pitcher turned into what looked like black gold in a matter of seconds, as it dripped through the mud and descended into his worn mug. It's safe to say Gee liked his coffee strong.

Lex strolled into the recreation room from morning program, his face acting as a thermometer for all to read. It looked cold out. He saw Gee in the corner by the microwave, headed straight over to him.

"Gee, you got that laundry I did for you last night, right?" he asked as he breathed deeply, trying to catch his breath.

Gee turned toward Lex, with his strainer in hand. "Yeah, I got it. It was all bunched-up and wrinkled in the bag though. I had to spend a half-hour this morning just ironing everything. I don't pay you so I can spend another half-hour fixing what I paid you to do in the first place," Gee told Lex.

Lex just stared at him for a moment. It was clear his emotions were at conflict with his reason. His emotions won.

"Well you know what then, fuck your clothes. You're always complaining about something. No one else has a problem with how I do the laundry but you. Fuck you and your clothes, Gee! You're just a bitch anyway!" Lex exclaimed, as he turned and headed toward the sleeping area of the dorm.

Gee was stunned and grew red with rage. He placed the strainer and his cup down on the table, and quickly followed Lex.

"ON THE COUNT, SITTING OR STANDING IN YOUR CUBES," Officer Torrent broadcast over the dorm's PA system, as Lex entered the sleeping area.

Officer Torrent was the afternoon officer on the unit. She was diminutive in stature, but a goliath if you got on her bad side. And many had gotten on her bad side, only to vanish off to solitary confinement for long stretches of time. She got up from the officer's station, and headed back out of the sleeping area. She always did this at count time, to check the bathroom and shower for stragglers. Gee passed her as he headed into the sleeping area close behind Lex. As soon as Officer

Torrent was in the recreation room, Gee started to run after Lex, who now saw Gee behind him and began to run himself...in the opposite direction.

"You motherfucker! Bitch huh? I'll show you bitch, you little punk-ass motherfucker," Gee yelled as he ran after Lex.

Lex kept ahead of him though, running around the perimeter of the sleeping area labyrinth with the noticeable advantage of someone half Gee's age.

"Yo, yo, she's coming. Police! Police!" another inmate yelled, as the sentry was close to return.

"I'll get you after, you fucking punk. You better bring your shank too, motherfucker, cause I'm gonna cut you up real good!" Gee yelled to Lex, as he turned and began to walk nonchalantly back to his cube.

Gee was overflowing with rage, with enmity...with a deep-seated desire to avenge this verbal affront. The utter disrespect Gee was paid by this kid half his age— in front of everyone in the recreation room—could not go unaddressed. Not in prison.

Officer Torrent came back into the sleeping area of the dorm, scanning the wide-open barracks. There was unease in the air; you could almost smell the insta-bility. She seemed to know something was afoot. Cor-rectional officers are trained to look for symptoms of a brewing conflict. Some even develop a sixth sense for recognizing a situation before it reaches a head.

She just stood there, looking around at the faces of a chorus in complicity. But she didn't have enough. A hunch was never enough to even initiate an investigation these days. Inmates had become just as litigious as the rest of society. Jailhouse lawyers had flooded the market, always looking for a grievance or lawsuit to file. There were new procedures now, new protocol, new standards for probable cause. The State had suffered too many losses to Article 78 motions, Federal 1983 actions and other civil suits. The hunch had been rendered just that—a hunch.

Officer Torrent completed her count of the inmates in the dorm, and then cleared the count—as always. Was she so surprised there was no one missing? There was never anyone missing. She turned to leave the sleeping area to go talk to the neighboring dorm officer, until the facility-wide count was cleared over the PA system. Gee knew this was the time...he had to be ready.

He wished he hadn't said what he did, at least about the shank. He remembered he gave his twelve-inch machete to a friend in another dorm to hold for him. If Lex had a shank and brought one to fight with, now he'd be the one in trouble. He had to do something. He would make the next best thing to the prison shank: the correctional mace. This is a medieval-like bludgeon made by simply placing a lock or a can of food in the bottom of a sock, tying it off, and using the length of the sock's remainder as a handle to swing the deadly weight at the end.

Gee fashioned one within minutes, and was ready. His heart was beating dangerously fast. He remembered taking his heart medication earlier, and hoped it wouldn't fail him now. He put away the coffee filter and strainer. As he locked up his belongings in his locker, it came. He saw it coming out of the corner of his eye. He pulled back to swing the mace, right as Lex's fist landed directly on his jaw. He started to fall back with the force of the blow, but the motion of his arm was resolute. The end of the mace followed through and struck Lex in the neck, just missing its intended target, which would have probably ended the dispute and Lex's consciousness right then and there.

Lex is now furious at Gee's attempt. He charges him, knocks him to the ground of his own cube. Lex gets on top of him, and unleashes his youthful fury. He lays punch after punch into Gee's weathered face, until Gee finally manages to thrust the fifty-pound differential into irrelevance. They struggle and toss on the cube's floor. Gee throws Lex against the small locker. The clash of steel into concrete reverberates through the captive dorm. Everyone is watching now. Everyone is transfixed on this no-holds-barred UFC match unfolding in ten-cube.

This was the lurking threat that has Gee on edge constantly, the threat that hid behind every corner. Gee knew better than anyone, that in prison, violence was the default mechanism to resolve disputes. He knew this was the way you settled things in here… no peaceful reasoning, no reconciliation, no other way. There is the fist, the mace and the shank. That's it. If you aren't able to swallow your pride, and brush off an affront or show of disrespect, then this is what happens. This is how conflicts get resolved. Blood is shed. The victor is elevated, the defeated departed. Sometimes they'd leave in cuffs, sometimes on a stretcher. Sometimes it's both.

The struggle continues. The crowd has now descended to get a closer view. Lex is getting the better of Gee, and is on top of him again. Lex's weight advantage is taking a toll on Gee's ability to defend.

"Police! Police is at the door! Chill! Chill!" someone yells from the crowd.

Lex immediately jumps up and runs out of Gee's cube, and back to the relative safety of his own. Everyone else disperses with haste. Gee slowly rises from below the disguise of the partition that separates the inmate cubes, visibly defeated. His face is red, and his left eye swollen shut. He's bleeding from his right cheek. There appears to be a laceration above his other eye.

Moments later, the roving officer came into the dorm from his walkway patrol and scanned the landscape. He knew something was afoul; he didn't merely have a hunch like Officer Torrent did. He was coming into the dorm when the ambush began, when Lex sucker-punched Gee without warning—without notice—in dirty fashion, typical of prison confrontation. Gee knew there were no rules in here, no parameters, no commonly accepted code of ethics or standard of behavior. He knew an act of disrespect was dealt with according to the slighted. It's handled based on the individual's propensity for violence, on his tolerance for this verbal offensive. He knew from all his time spent in prison that you have to be prepared for anything, at any time. Once it rose to this level, the beef didn't end until the parties left under the guidance of the powerful hand of administration...either in closer custody en route to solitary confinement, or under white coat supervision on a stretcher.

The roving officer began to walk the dormitory's perimeter, scanning faces and looking for clues of a struggle. He knows the approximate area of the fracas; Gee's cube was right next to the window by the door he entered through. The roving officer had heard some commotion from outside by the door. When he came in, he could instantly tell. His presumption had been confirmed: violence was in the air.

He got to Gee's cube, stopping right in front. Gee was sitting on his chair. He was combing his hair, peering into what he hoped would be taken for a mirror lodged deep in the recesses of his locker. But the officer knew something was askew. Even if there was a mirror in there, Gee's stare seared right through it. He was almost looking into another dimension, far past the vanity of his battered likeness. That's what adrenaline does.

"Mr. Luna, how are we doing today?" the officer asked, as Gee's stare stayed fixed in his locker.

He knows he can't ignore the officer.

"Mr. Luna..." the officer repeats.

"Oh, hey, Officer Culello, what's going on?" Gee answered, slowly turning toward him.

It was no use trying to hide his face; only speaking in the opposite direction would save him now, and that wasn't an option. Gee had no choice but to explain his way out of this now.

"What happened to your face, Mr. Luna?" Officer Culello asked.

He looked him straight in the eye, hoping his time as a former worker under Officer Culello down at the gym might buy him a reprieve, maybe some leniency.

"Well...Mr. Culello, you're gonna laugh. It's kinda funny actually. I smashed my face with the door to my locker...it swings open pretty hard sometimes, damn door," he said to the officer.

Officer Culello just stood there, examining Gee's face, his injuries, and noting how entirely inconsistent they were with the capability of an unwieldy locker door, no matter how cumbrous.

"All right, Mr. Luna, all right," he said as he headed back to the officer's station. He got on the phone immediately. Gee knew he was calling the area sergeant, he knew he was caught. But there was nothing he could do now. It was only a matter of time, but it was always just a matter of time in prison. Someone always got caught, though...the aggressor or the beaten, and often both.

The dorm was kept in suspension, swaying with the incertitude of a poorly engineered bridge. The usual murmur of prison small talk had fallen to a whisper. Inmates had huddled around various cubes, quietly discussing how the beef would unfold; when the fuzz would arrive; who would be most likely to snitch and rat the other one out, because that almost always happened. Gee knew that if it wasn't one of the parties actually involved in the beef, it'd be some unassuming inmate or confidential informant dropping a slip to the authorities.

Not five minutes after Officer Culello got off the phone, the enforcement of correctional policy began. The area sergeant and five accompanying officers descended on the dorm.

"Everyone to their cubes, NOW!" the sergeant yelled across the tiled expanse as he entered.

Anyone who wasn't already in his cube made his way back there quickly.

"Two of my officers are going to walk around and check hands and faces for bruises," he announced, as two of the correctional officers departed down opposite aisles.

They began inspecting, until one officer got to Lex's cube, and stopped. He seemed to be hung up on something, but then he continued—right past the guilty man. It was obvious Lex was certainly no tenderfoot when it came to prison conflict. He had worn a pair of weightlifting gloves when he attacked Gee. The gloves absorbed the brunt of the abrasion that hard blows from the fist usually produce, masking any evidence he'd been a party to the fight.

The other officer was now firmly entrenched at the threshold to ten-cube, which is Gee's cube. He's interrogating Gee. Gee wasn't as lucky as Lex: unfortunately there is no equivalent to the glove that can be used as a mask for the face in combat. The officer called over the sergeant. They exchanged words quietly. The dorm was now silent in anticipation, save this low conversation in the corner. It was obvious the uniforms were making no progress. Gee was too seasoned in this to be intimidated by the authorities, especially in plain view of everyone else. He stuck solidly by his locker door story.

The sergeant gathered his men. They spoke for a few minutes out in the recreation room, as everyone watched intently from the perch of his cube. Then the cadre of blue men left. They left empty-handed, their extra shackles still shining with vacancy. Disappointment could be seen in their departure; their tight grip sans the flesh expectant.

The dorm officer released the cube-hold order, and allowed for normal activity and movement about the dorm to resume again. Just minutes later, the phone rang.

"Inmate Luna, ten-cube, report to the officer's bubble immediately," the officer broadcast over the loudspeaker.

Gee knew what was in store; he'd been in this situation before. He locked up his locker, and headed to the officer's station. The exchange was quiet and brief.

"Mr. Luna, you need to report to the sergeant's office in the activity building, NOW," the officer told Gee.

Gee nodded in acquiescence, not needing to say anything. He turned and headed out of the dorm, as everyone watched and wondered.

Everyone knew this is when the authorities tried to get you to squeal, to snitch, to rat out the other party. They did this while you were sequestered temporarily from the merciless masses, in the transitory safety of the unfriendly government office. They'd do this as if it wouldn't catch up with you later if you talked. Just because someone is in prison, doesn't mean they're stupid. Most understood the false safety, and knew the ramifications of loose lips. No one knew this better than Gee. Everyone knew Gee would stand firm, wouldn't give up Lex's name when interrogated. Gee was a lifer. He'd been in prison over thirty years already on a murder charge. He was an Original Gangster, an OG as they say. He was pure old school. He'd spent twenty years in the maximum security prisons across the state. He'd seen what happens to snitches. He'd seen the rat-hunters at work, and he knew what they did to snitches.

Gee came back to the dorm just as quick as he'd left. He was only gone maybe fifteen minutes. He went straight to his cube. Afternoon program was about to go out, carrying the bulk of the dorm with it, Gee and Lex included.

Lex had now become visibly worried. Gee was back on the dorm unit. They hadn't detained him. It was beginning to sink in for Lex, the ramifications of attacking someone such as Gee, who was doing a life sentence and didn't have nearly as much to lose as he did. Gee had already killed somebody to bring him to prison. Fuck. He was getting scared now at what Gee might do in retaliation. Lex didn't merely disrespect Gee once, but he did it three times. He called Gee a bitch, he sucker-punched him, and then he entered the sacrosanct area of Gee's cube and proceeded to beat him unawares. None of these acts would or could go unpunished in prison, in a world governed first by the absolutes of respect, and then by the hand of administration.

Somehow, the rest of the day was quiet. Lex and Gee managed to avoid each other…but the beef wasn't over. Everyone was talking about it, wondering what would happen, what Gee will do in response. The anxiety was thick. The day approached expiration, but nothing happened. The other inmates began to shift their focus, and move their attention to their own concerns. The day was almost over, and the last count was taken. The uncertainty of the darkness engulfed the dorm, as the lights were extinguished. Anything could happen now.

But somehow, nothing did. The morning count came, with the relative assurance of the stadium lighting coming to life. Both parties were present and accounted for…with no new, undocumented wounds.

Good had won over evil. Good had notched a lonely win in the left column, but a resounding win, nonetheless! After Gee got back from the sergeant's interrogation, he went to his cube to think. He wanted to be by himself; to contemplate his options, to decide on his course of action. He thought of his family, of how he'd been apart from them for over three decades already. He thought of how he'd watched his children grow old from prison, through an occasional letter or holiday visit. He thought of how he'd never even met his grandchildren. He thought of all the family he'd lost to death since he'd been gone. All of this saddened him, and made him regretful about what he'd done so long ago to bring him to this wretched cesspool of existence. He decided right then and there what he was going to do: he was going to do nothing.

Gee would let the beef die. He would take the disrespect and keep it moving, as they say. He'd take the beating and heal. Gee wasn't going to let some young punk get the best of him, and possibly cause him to get a new charge. He wasn't going to let Lex be the reason he was sent to solitary confinement, or jeopardize his already long odds at his next parole board hearing. No, not this time. Maybe ten years ago, maybe even two years ago. But not this year, not today, not now. Gee was going to do the right thing, finally, putting an end to a long line of doing the wrong thing.

The respect he commanded among the other inmates in the compound would suffer, his correctional stature would falter. Lex's would strengthen, his station rise. But none of this seemed to bother Gee anymore. He wasn't concerned with how other prisoners viewed him, he was concerned with how his family viewed him.

Later that morning, both Gee and Lex were moved to different dorms. Someone had dropped an anonymous slip the night before to the authorities and told them what had really happened. Both Gee and Lex went their separate ways, each carrying with him a sense of victory. But Gee's victory meant so much more. It was the prize hardly anyone else sought, but one which was infinitely more valuable.

AGAINST THE CURRENT

We hadn't really talked, except maybe once or twice. There was the occasional head bow, a door held slightly beyond expectation, but nothing of any real import. I'd been sitting in my crudely fashioned stopgap—the two tables and my Smith Corona typewriter I liked to call my "office." He went by the name Lex, which I would later come to find out was just short for his government name, Alexi. I made the mistake of calling him by his real name once. At the third syllable I was met with a pointed scowl, told to never call him by that again. Right. Lex. Sorry.

He approached the tables in the rear corner of the recreation room, stopped in front of the typewriter. I looked up from my work, as he asked if he could interrupt. This was one of those "courtesies" that didn't entertain the possibility of a denial. Sure, I said, by default. He seemed to be contemplating how to phrase what he wanted to say. He quickly gathered, and looked up from the table to meet my eyes.

"You know, I've been thinking, and observing... and I wanted to know if you noticed the same thing," he said as I stared intently.

"Out of a dorm of fifty-five inmates, you seem to be the only person actually putting in the work to better yourself. Everyone else in here is just killing time, waiting for their release day so they can go back to their lives, and head right back to prison soon after," he said, as my curious expression turned to one more solemn.

I nodded gravely, and told him I did share in this observation, and was reminded daily of its tragedy.

"I mean, these dudes just play chess, checkers, dominos, make bowls of food three times normal portion, and watch the same music videos and Sportscenter re-runs every day. But when you ask them what they're doing to try and address why they're in prison and what they're gonna do when they get out, they have these big ass explanations and master plans...yet they're not doing shit in here!" he exclaimed, growing more passionate with every sentence.

I could only nod, as it echoed my own sentiment and lament.

"Don't you see this, man? This is a fucking problem! What the hell is wrong with these dudes?" Lex asked, as his normally flat eyes peeled wide.

"Somebody's gotta do something man; this shit is fuckin' crazy!" he said.

"I know what you mean, Lex. I know," I told him in response.

We talked for a few minutes before they called the midday chow run. About solutions, about where the heart of the problem lay. But ultimately we reached no consensus. We reached no grand cure, no plan to try to address this sad reality. We simply shared a similar opinion, and bemoaned an atmosphere and a culture removed from the mainstream, one largely neglected and obscured by the larger cultural apparatus of society.

In the days that followed this conversation, I found Lex approaching me with less hesitation. Where there was once the reservation used with a foreigner, now there was the familiarity akin to allies. He viewed me as an oasis, a beacon of sorts. We began to talk more, share ideas and discuss various things. He asked to borrow some of my books. I lent him books on ancient Greek philosophy, modern European history, and a few works of classic literature from the twentieth century American canon. He asked me if I'd help tutor him so he could finally pass and get his GED. I agreed, and we began tutorials immediately. Lex started to really follow my lead down the path not often taken in here. I was proud. I was proud of him, and of my fortunate position as a leader and a mentor.

Over the following weeks, I saw Lex move further and further away from the steady current of the prison abyss. He gradually began to stay in his cell more. He spent less time bullshitting and watching TV, and more time reading and studying in his cell. This was encouraging, especially juxtaposed against the steadily unsettling behavior of my neighbor, a certain individual nicknamed CanDo.

CanDo was a leader in all the wrong ways. He was a bit like the Speaker of the House, representing his fellow inmates in the Congress of Convicts. But he was a corrupt, conniving leader. He was a "Big Homie," which meant he was high up in rank in the powerful gang of the Bloods. He commanded respect from his fellow gang members, the "Lil Homies," as well as other inmates, through fear and intimidation. He was a Lieutenant in the organization he claimed membership of, and was one of the most dangerous inmates in this facility. And he was my neighbor, slept three feet from my head.

His physical presence alone elicited fear and unease. He stood about six-foot-five, and had to weigh at least two-sixty, maybe two-seventy. He was cut-up, too. The dude worked out twice a day. The first thing you saw wasn't his face, it was his chest, protruding like a mantel capable of balancing a glass of water without worry. This guy could probably collapse a face with one solid blow, and I'd heard several stories of how he had. Naturally, I knew it was in my best interest to get on this guy's good side. This is exactly what I did.

We got along, well enough at least. He'd tell me of his upbringing constantly, how he'd grown up with nothing in the Queensbridge projects of New York City. He must have reminded me weekly of this fact, as if I'd forgotten somehow. He'd tell me how he'd risen to the top ranks of the notorious Bloods; how he'd thrown bricks of cocaine weekly; how he'd bed a different girl every night. The stories fell in flurries: it'd be clear for a week, then I'd be buried in a narrative blizzard. They were often spun like fiction, and most of it probably was. But I nodded and smiled, gave props and kudos where appropriate. You gotta fake it to make it sometimes, especially in prison.

At first our neighborly relationship was nothing more than these exchanges and reminisces. I regarded and respected CanDo out of necessity and the instinct to survive. But I gradually saw what he was really made of, what his character was really composed of, and the fabric wasn't strong. CanDo would begin each day with a somewhat cursory read of some section of the Bible. He would end each day the same way. The problem or inconsistency with this sat squarely in the middle: during the day, his actions and attitude showed a complete disregard for everything the Bible stands for. This is no exaggeration. The glaring hypocrisy was halting, yet certain.

CanDo was a hustler by nature, seemed to have been brought up that way in the urban jungle of Queensbridge. His rackets grew alongside his frame. He began as a petty thief; quickly moved up the larceny ladder to jacking whips; grand theft auto at age fourteen; segued to the drug trade when the heat rose. This proved the most lucrative of enterprises he'd seen. When this wasn't enough, he moved into the strong-arm market. Instead of just dealing, he also began simply taking, whether you liked it or not.

Most didn't like it, but could do nothing to stop it, unless getting pistol whipped happened to be on their to-do list that day.

When he was locked up on this current bid, for robbery in the first, he'd simply been relocated in his criminal organization. CanDo immediately linked up with his fellow Bloods once he hit the cool concrete of the penitentiary yard. They exchanged war stories, shared conquest tales of their endless bedroom prowess, and they put him up on the local block in the joint. Within weeks after hitting reception, he was doing what he'd always done on the street: hustling and trying to get over on others. The only difference was he'd just been demoted a few rungs in terms of serviceable markets. Instead of dealing in serious weight—kilos and such—he was now throwing grams. Instead of wielding double barrel shotguns by Mossberg, he was now packing double razors by Bic fashioned to a shank. The market had changed, the medium had changed, but the mode was the same. The mode was the problem.

As the weeks progressed, CanDo's faux-religiosity only got worse. He started to quote Psalms, and read whole passages of Judges to me. He even had the gall to tell me I should be reading the Bible. It was hard not to say anything, but I remained silent. One day CanDo came back from a disciplinary hearing, with fourteen days loss of recreation as punishment. This meant he had to spend those fourteen days confined to his sleeping area, directly next to mine. I cringed. I knew it was going to be a long fourteen days.

As the days went on, though, I was pleasantly surprised. I was introduced to a whole new CanDo. The dramaturgy of his life in the streets and in prison was at intermission. When the histrionics ceased, a different side of CanDo emerged. I was confused at first, taken aback. Was this simply all an act? He began to read with a verve formerly unknown. He asked me for books every day, engaged me in conversation—not bullshitting, but conversation. I was impressed and relieved at once. I thought I'd maybe misjudged his character after all. Maybe the criminal mind was influenced more by nurture and less by nature. Maybe.

One conversation in particular between us stood out. It was late one night, maybe a Friday or Saturday. CanDo had been quiet all day: thinking, reading, writing. He spoke unlike I'd ever heard him speak before. Candid observation, remorse and dreams of a better life are what he talked of. He spoke of how this "human warehousing" thing of prison was crazy, and yet he kept coming back to it. Did he like it here? Why was he back for the third time now? He told me how he'd spent eleven of the past fourteen years behind bars. He was thirty-two, his youth officially over, wasted, drained of any realization. He couldn't do this anymore. Not him, not away from his family, his three kids. No, not anymore, he said.

It was a surprise to see him, O.D. that is. I hadn't seen O.D. in over a month, which was unusual in this small compound. He came right up to me, eyes wide with a bright smile on his face.

"Well, what the hell! It's about time I run into you," he said as we hit the hammer and gave the old prison pat on the back.

I'd been walking the yard when he spotted me. He bee-lined across the grassy expanse to meet my grueling stride. I told him to walk with me...let's talk and catch up.

O.D. was a reserved but colorful fellow. We'd met that summer playing on opposing teams in the Cayuga Cup, the penitentiary's highly distilled version of the World Cup. He'd never played soccer before, but picked it up quicker than most I'd seen among the "prison athletes," those who'd rarely if ever played any sports prior to coming to prison. O.D. was a natural athlete. He was six-two, one-ninety. His vertical had to be over three feet. He could dunk with ease not seen in someone six inches his better.

We walked and we talked. O.D. told me how well things were coming along with the book he'd been writing. He bounced off various thematic ideas and plot twists, for which I gave him my opinion. He spoke of his intention to enroll in the upcoming Cornell University college courses offered here at the facility, and how he was going to get a foundation in here over the next couple of years, and then go to college when he gets out. He threw various business ideas my way too, looking for advice and counsel, feedback and rapport.

I always loved talking with O.D. Our conversations made me smile and lifted my spirit. His positive attitude—his determination to grow and change—was refreshing. He stood apart from the majority in prison. Through sheer will and determination, O.D. was able to find a sandbar, pull himself up, and watch the current of vice and sin sweep away soul after soul. He refused to take the easy path anymore. He'd been letting this current pull him his whole life, and it brought him right to the gates of prison...deposited him like silt in a delta. But he had fought the urge to drown, to give in to the norms and the expected. And his words weren't merely words: they were fortified with action, deeds and substance. O.D. was a correctional pariah.

It had barely been a month, maybe only three weeks. Lex had been making such wonderful progress, and then it happened: a regression of sorts. A misunderstanding is where it began; a fractured arm, bruised knuckles, and the twisted satisfaction from an opponent's pummeled face is where it ended. Lex got into a brutal fight with Gee, an older lifer on the unit, because of some laundry dispute. It was bullshit, something about the laundry being wrinkled. Petty, but it was this pettiness that was usually the root of most confrontation in here, because life is largely petty in prison. The small things are what matter, and they're governed by the implacable norm of respect and respect only.

Lex's old, grotesque side had found its way back to the forefront, and it was hideous. It was violent and it was destructive. But this wasn't the most disturbing part. More unnerving was how easily this violence was administered—by default, with no contemplation, no consideration. All of the desire to change, all of the tutorials, all of the time spent staying in his cell and reading, was now lost. It was gone in an instant, defeated by a conditioning too strong to suppress.

The fourteen days punishment went by quicker than I'd expected. CanDo got off loss of recreation punishment and, without delay, headed back out to the recreation room with head held high and his affected swagger in full stride. It was as if he hadn't missed a beat. He strode right over to the TV, changed the channel from the movie six guys had been watching, and settled on a music video he'd probably seen a hundred times, without asking anyone.

"Yo, what the fuck? We were watchin that," someone said from the bench.

"Oh yeah? Well we're watchin this now. You got a problem with that? Say somethin..." CanDo begged, pining for a challenge.

He'd been out of the action and on a timeout for two weeks now. He was eager to reassert his position on the dorm as the *guy you don't fuck with,* especially now that we'd gotten a few new jacks on the unit in the meantime. CanDo didn't want any of them getting any ambitious ideas. He ran the show.

Within days, CanDo was set back up on the yard hustling, just like before. He was risking everything— his life, more time on top of his sentence, his family— all for a few extra dollars, which might buy a few extra drumsticks of chicken on the commissary or maybe some Swiss Rolls. It took no real fight, no struggle, to resist the pull of the current for CanDo. He was pulled right back into the negativity of the general inmate population, like an addict is to his drug of choice. All of his vows, his admissions, his resolutions, were forgotten.

"Well, well, well...twice in two weeks, now that's a first," O.D. said with a smile, as we ran into each other in the weight pit.

"What are you doing here? I thought you worked out at two?" I asked.

"I do usually, but the words were flowing earlier, so I didn't want to mess that up and stop writing," O.D replied.

"Yo, I read your essay in the facility's publication," he added.

"I thought it was amazing and right-on. It was so inspiring, I sat down and started to work on my own essay. It's on the adolescent development of one troubled youth from the projects of the Bronx, Webster Ave., where I grew up. You think you could read it when I'm done? Maybe help me edit it?" he asked with eyes wide and eager.

"Sure, I'd love to help you, O.D.," I told him.

He went on to tell me how his book had been coming. He'd finished three chapters since we last talked. He said he'd sent in his application for the Cornell college courses. They were offering a pre-law course and one in anthropology, which he was particularly excited about. He didn't know if he'd like the law course on individual rights and the Constitution, but thought it was a good idea to take it anyway. I agreed.

"You think you can give me a quick spot on the bench press?" O.D. asked, as we neared the recreation movement to head back to the dorms for the facility count.

"Yeah, let's hurry up though; they're about to call an end to recreation time," I told him, as he lay under what appeared—after a hasty addition—to be a little over three hundred pounds.

"Damn, O.D., that's 315, you know," I cautioned him before I lifted it off the bench press rack.

"Yeah, I know. I've been putting some time in out here. What, you can't tell by looking at me? Shit...I got my game up, son!" he said as he lifted the weight off the rack singlehandedly.

He proceeded to press four reps, before I even lent any assistance to complete the set of six.

"Well, I guess you did. Damn! Nice set, O.D." I told him, as he racked the weight and escaped the stubbornness of that looming barbell.

He had gotten his strength up indeed, and not just in the weight pit. O.D. had set goals for himself while he was imprisoned. He'd made commitments and resolutions, and now he was putting in the work necessary to make his dreams a reality. O.D. understood words without action are meaningless, and faith without works is dead.

He refused to be another statistic, another example of why recidivism demands more prisons, higher walls, and longer bids. No, he was not going to let the correctional rip tide pull him under. This was his first and last time in shackles. He knew he didn't have to return, if he didn't want to return. But it began now, in here, with his attitude and his behavior. This was his life, and he refused to let anyone tell him when to eat, when to sleep, and when to shower anymore. It ended here, and it began here. O.D. knew this truth, this truth so few know, and it empowered him.

O.D. was in prison, but he was free. He was as free as a bird, to fly the skies of possibility, of redemption and opportunity. He'd chosen the path less traveled, and bucked the trend of comfort. He was going to be okay, he was going to make it. Although he was locked up, he'd never been more free.

THE CURIOUS CIRCUMVENTION
OF THE COPY CALAMITY
A CAUTIONARY TALE

They had called the six-thirty recreation movement early. But it didn't matter, because I was ready. I flew out of the dormitory gate like Secretariat at the Preakness, was the first one on the path toward the prize. I guess it's not much of a prize though, come to think of it. Being the first one to the Law Library to make copies? What was the rush anyhow? I often found myself asking this question, as I would move with haste on the facility movements. After all, all I have is time. But why do people speed when they drive? To shave a mere five minutes off the commute? Not usually. It's more hardwiring, part of one's disposition and one's personality. Why waste time when you can save time? I believe it's more First-In-First-Out (FIFO) than Last-In-First-Out (LIFO), to make a bad accounting analogy.

Others began to trickle out of the their dormitories, the small tributary paths flowing into the main channel of inmate traffic. I was out in front, folder in hand. I was going to make copies of the most recent short story I had written. I had just finished writing the sixth piece only hours before, and I wanted to send it home in the morning mail pick-up tomorrow, in case I was searched and the authorities found it. I flashed my ID to the officer at the Activity Building door, and he motioned me through. I entered, and headed down the long hallway to the Law Library.

As I walked in, I noticed it wasn't the regular officer, Ms. Joyce. It must be a fill-in, I thought. He sat at the officer's desk behind the counter in the back by the windows. He was reading the newspaper. As I approached the counter, I realized who it was: it was Officer Dumas. I had heard a lot about this guy, and none of it good. I'd heard how he was cantankerous at best, and downright dangerous at worst. I had seen him in action a few times, but was luckily never the target of his capricious wrath.

I reached the counter with caution and noticeable reservation. He could definitely see that I was standing there, folder in hand, but he didn't even look up. We were the only two in the library. It was a warm evening, and most had probably postponed their legal work and deferred the reality of their lives for the ephemeral Band-Aid of the recreation yard. I waited twenty, maybe even thirty seconds. There was still no acknowledgement of my presence. I had to break the silence, broach some sort of dialogue with this guy.

"Excuse me, Officer, I have my approved disbursement form to pay for forty pages of copies. I need two copies of this document," I said, as his eyes slowly rose from the paper to meet mine.

There was silence...an uncomfortable stretch of nothingness. He just stared at me, like I had asked him to open the front gate of the prison so I could walk free. He stared, and stared, like I was crazy.

Finally, he asked, "Why didn't you come at one, or two, or three-thirty for the copies?"

I told him because you're allowed to come to make copies on any recreation movement. I had been busy at the other times, which is why I was coming now in the evening.

He reluctantly rose from the oversized chair he so clearly exceeded. He walked over to the counter where I was standing, visibly annoyed. He asked for the disbursement-of-funds receipt and my ID. I handed him both. He examined both with unusual attention, foreign care almost. He placed them on the counter.

"For one, Weimer, I don't work for you. You got that? You don't just come in here and say 'yo guy, I need two copies of this,' you got that?" He leaned into my face.

"That's not how this works. I got ten years in corrections; that shit ain't working with me, pal," he said, as I just stared at him.

"But I never said 'Yo guy'; I said 'excuse me, Officer'..." I replied.

"No you didn't! You came in here, with some entitlement bullshit, like I gotta do something for you. Well, fuck that! You wait for me! I address you! That is when and if I'm ready, and only then maybe I'll consider making the copies. In fact, gimme the folder," he said, his anger rising.

I handed him the folder with my sixth short story in it. He opened it, flipped through the story quickly. He read a few lines, then looked up at me.

"What the fuck is this? This isn't legal work?" he said. "What is this crap?" he asked again.

"I know, but I never said it was legal work. I'm just making copies of a story I wrote. I've been doing this with Officer Joyce for months now…" I offered in defense.

"I don't care what you've been doing with Officer Joyce. She's not here, is she? I'm here now. This is my library, and look what it says right here on your disbursement receipt: Legal Copies. This isn't legal work! These aren't legal copies! You can only make LEGAL COPIES in the Law Library. What the fuck is wrong with you?" he says to me in disgust.

I just stare at him, wondering the exact same thing about him. What the hell is wrong with this guy? Why is he getting so angry? Why is he raising his voice, targeting me for no real reason?

Before I can even say anything in rebuttal to this belligerence, he says,

"You know what? I'm not gonna make the copies. You don't like it? File a grievance, and see how that goes. You wanna come in here all gung-ho, into my library, saying hey, guy, I need copies, when clearly you see I'm busy. I gotta run this whole library you know, by myself. I'm a very busy guy. If everyone just comes in here wanting copies of their latest best seller, how am I supposed to do my job? Huh?"

I'm speechless at this point. I mean, what do you say to this? What can you say to this? I knew what I wanted to say: This "whole" library? You mean the one with only one other person in it, who needs two copies that will take all of thirty seconds? Or shall we discuss how "busy" you really are. Is that newspaper becoming burdensome? Are the job responsibilities holding you back? This is what I thought and wanted to say, but I knew better. I couldn't say any of this. I was smarter than that. I had to appease the irrationality, and placate the unreasoned aggression.

"You know what, forget it. This is ridiculous. I'll come back another day," I told him as I took my folder and headed for the door.

"I hope you do come back another day—to prison, that is. Thanks for the job security, asshole," Officer Dumas said as I left the library.

He said this with such prejudicial enmity—such spite—that it made me slow my departure. I desperately wanted to turn back to respond. I wanted so bad to say what was on my mind, what was on the tip of my tongue: *you better thank God for that job security, because with your skill set and attitude, you'd be earning one-fourth the salary with no benefits, were it not for this "busy job" of yours.* But I didn't say anything. Prudence overpowered pride. I kept thinking of my family, of my still-tenuous parole date to go home. I turned back around, closed the door, and proceeded down the hall.

* * *

I'm sitting in my usual seat, in the back corner of the small group room. It's the first room on your right when you enter the Activity Building. There's a thick glass window to the hallway, so the Officers can keep an eye on us, in case our fellowship meeting gets out of hand, too raucous to contain. I've heard coffee changes people. All of a sudden, who do I see pass by, only to back peddle when he spots me? Officer Dumas. You gotta be kidding me. He stares straight at me through the pane. I try not to make eye contact, but I do. He beckons for me to come out in the hallway. I raise my arms, to signal I'm clearly busy and in the middle of a meeting. His look turns more grave, and he gives me another more stern beckon with the index and middle finger.

The group I'm in senses danger. It voices its concern, but I wave it off. I have to deal with this myself and face this guy alone. I walk out of the room, to meet Officer Dumas in the hallway. He asks me what I'm doing.

"What am I doing? What does it look like I'm doing?" I mistakenly say with a noticeable attitude.

"I'm trying to get some recovery talk in my meeting here. Is that all right?" I sense my slip as the words leave my mouth.

"So you're a smart ass too, huh? All right. You know what, I'll deal with you later. Come down to the Law Library when the meeting's over at 8:30. We'll talk then. I'll think about what I'm going to do with you until then," he tells me, turning to walk away before I can say anything.

As I returned to our meeting, the usual comfort and solace was absent. I began to get a little worried. The next half hour of the meeting was extremely nerve-racking. I was now in serious jeopardy of going to the hoosegow, also known as solitary confinement in here. My fate was at the mercy of this one person, this one officer of the State. Unfortunately, due process of law does not always get the attention it deserves in the correctional clime, and this can become a problem when you're an inmate of the State.

This is an injustice for the persecuted inmates, and for the many correctional officers of good character and moral pedigree whom this behavior reflects poorly on. It must be made clear that Officer Dumas is an exception, that he's an outlier to the statistical mean of security temperament. The vast majority of uniformed correctional officers whom I've met, and been under direct custody of, are reasonable people. They are law-abiding, taxpaying citizens of our great country. They serve a vital role in society, striving to protect the public, and advance the rehabilitation of the wayward. It is a shame a few must tarnish the reputation of the many.

The meeting came to a close sooner than I would have liked. It was 8:30, and they just called recreation movement back to the dormitories. I had to go see Officer Dumas and learn of my immediate fate. But I'm supposed to go to work in five minutes as a recreation aide in the weight pit. How am I going to talk to him, make it back to the dorm, change and make it back out to the yard all in the next five minutes? This was impossible, I thought.

I shake everyone's hand and bid my farewell until our next meeting. This could either be in two days, or thirty-two days if things don't go well and I visit solitary confinement à la Officer Dumas. I leave the room and head toward the Law Library. By this point, my anger over this officer's strengthening whim has yielded to a rising worry rooted deep in my solar plexus; an anxiety that is ripe with precedent and potentiality. I know what this guy's capable of, and I've heard what he's done. I've seen what he's gotten away with, how just days earlier he had slammed an inmate's head into the wall, and thrown his legal work across the floor, all because the inmate objected to Dumas's beyond-cursory reading of his privileged legal mail.

I entered the Law Library with renewed humility, walked in with a fresh perspective. But it was for naught. The onslaught was prompt, before the door was even closed. He was perched and waiting like a gamecock champing at the bit, pining for the opening lunge.

"Well, well, well…if it isn't the guy who thinks he's entitled to something…the guy who thinks I work for him," he said as the silence was lost.

He proceeded to lay into a jumbled rant. He unleashed one verbal haymaker after another. I just stood there, not three feet from his ruddy face, absorbing the lexical offensive. I offered no defense, no justification and no minimization.

When he was finished, he handed me my ID back. He told me to come back to the Law Library tomorrow at 1:00 in the afternoon; he would have decided by then what to do with me. He had to look in the rulebook and research the infractions I was in violation of. He needed some time to further mull what he was going to do with me. Solitary confinement was still on the table, he reminded me. I took my ID, said nothing and left to head back to the dorm. My pride and disgust were practically choking me as I walked out of that room.

Just as ordered, I showed up at the Law Library the next afternoon at one o'clock. Officer Dumas was standing outside the door to the Activity Building, smoking with another officer whom I had seen but did not recognize at first.

"Hey John, look who it is; it's my new whipping boy. Me and Weimer are becoming good friends, aren't we, Weimer?" he asked with a sickening smile.

"I just think we got off to a rocky start, that's all. It was a simple miscommunication," I replied.

Officer Dumas ordered me to head to the Law Library in front of him, then added:

"He's like my red-headed stepchild, John. What the hell am I gonna do with him?" The other officer laughed, more out of amusement than empathy. I said nothing, as I walked toward the Law Library.

I enter the library, and proceed to the usual counter. Officer Dumas walks around me to the other side of the partition.

"Give me the little story you wrote, the one you want copies of," he says to me.

I hand him the folder with the story in it. He takes it and walks over to his desk. He sits down in his chair with his feet on the steel desk, opens the folder and begins to read my story.

"You can have a seat until I'm done," he directs me.

I pull a chair off the table, flip it over and sit. Immediately it hits me. Oh no! The story he's got is about a typical day in prison, told in the first person about my experience in this world of corrections. It's about my time at that particular facility, and I've naively included three officers who—in their own worthy characters— have warranted inclusion in the story. This normally wouldn't be a problem, except I pulled a rookie writer's mistake and forgot one of the cardinal betes noires of autobiographical authorship: change the names of real people unless you have their written permission. Fuck!!!

This blunder balloons in magnitude when you are incarcerated, and under the care, custody and control of those you have just disparaged. Yeah, I was in some serious shit should Officer Dumas get to the parts of the story where his fellow colleagues are mentioned; where they are portrayed in not the most favorable light, given their fraternity in the minority of "bad-apple" uniforms.

Stay calm, I told myself. Relax. Find a way to frustrate his interest in the story, and interrupt his attention. He continued to read. Now he's two, maybe three pages in, as I really start to worry now. Then he looks up at me.

"What the fuck, this story's about sailing? How lame. Where's the meat-and-potatoes of the story?" he asks me, clearly annoyed.

I see my opportunity. This is it, now run him off the road!

"Well, officer, that isn't one of my better stories. It's kind of slow, and a bit unexciting," I tell him in straight face.

"You don't say, huh?" he quips back.

He pulls the two pages he's read from the bottom of the stack, places the cluster haphazardly back into the folder, and throws it on his desk.

"Well that's enough of that, that sucked," he says, as his eyes rise to meet mine.

"So, where to begin. You're in violation of numerous rules, Weimer: Misleading an Officer; Misuse of State property; Defrauding the State; Causing a Disturbance; the list goes on and on," he tells me, his feet now resting firmly on top of my folder.

He calls over one of the Law Library inmate clerks. He tells him to explain to me what happened to the last inmate who came down here trying to make copies of a book he too was writing.

"Oh yeah, Jeffers. Yeah, they sent him to the box for thirty days...but we never actually saw him again after that. I don't know what happened to him really," the inmate clerk told me, with not a hint of solidarity or empathy in his demeanor.

He then turned and quickly resumed what he'd been doing, clearly wanting nothing to do with my situation. Wonderful, that's reassuring.

Officer Dumas got up from his chair and walked over to where I was now standing. He met me at the counter, pulled my ID card from his chest pocket, and handed it to me. Then he proceeded to issue a stern warning, and repeated the litany of charges he'd decided not to file. He told me this was mostly because of how he'd perceived a change in my attitude from yesterday to today, how this "reappearance" at the Court of Dumas was largely a test. This was his arbitrary and capricious test of attitude, demeanor and blind acquiescence to authority, no matter how that authority may be sometimes. It was a test I had thankfully passed today, one that had spared me a trip to solitary confinement for thirty days. The small price for this pass: the discipline to accept the things I cannot change, the courage to change the things I can, and the wisdom to know the difference. It was that easy.

Officer Dumas handed me the folder with my story in it.

"Oh yeah, and if I ever read a story someday in the unlikely chance you get this published, and come across a Mr. Asshole, or Officer Douche Bag, I'm gonna know you're writing about me. And believe me, I'll come after you, Weimer," he said as I took the folder and began to turn for the door.

I told him I wouldn't, but as soon as I got out of the Law Library and into the hallway, it hit me: I had to write a story about him. Not as an act of open defiance or rejection of authority, or out of a want of respect for the administration of the State. No. I needed to out of the very respect I have for authority, for law and order, for due process. It is precisely because of people like Officer Dumas that individuals' civil rights are infringed, or outright denied. It is dispositions like his that become corrupt and maligned with the vesting of the slightest amount of authority, even the smallest amount of power. It is abused, it is mistreated and misused, and all to the detriment of those under the authority.

This also degrades those in similar positions who carry the responsibility and duty with honor. I was savvy enough to re-evaluate, tack and change my strategy and approach. It allowed me to avoid a larger injustice. Unfortunately, many would not have or could not have taken the same path. Their pride, their sense of right and wrong, their ego may not have allowed it. They would have become victims, like others before me and like many to come. If I don't assume the responsibility, then who will? I have a duty and a responsibility to fight the billy club with the pen, and I always will.

A NEW YEAR

The division is sharp and decisive. Where the line is usually blurred, confusion's now impossible. Calm and reserved, or skittish and chatty. You belonged to one camp or the other, but only for tonight; only for this annual transition from a year past to one ahead. The sleeping area of the dorm was almost silent, but the recreation room was in a state of frenzy.

That worn telecast from Times Square fixed the attention of thirty men, under the direction of an equally spent host in the relic Dick Clark. But the program remained, and the interest increased. Groups of inmates formed among the recreation room masses—in the various corners, around the tables, under the TV. Grown men were singing along with the performing artists who'd bounce on and off the camera. Smiles had lost their normally rare status in here—they'd yielded to emotion and flooded the market...for the moment, anyway. If reality hadn't been so heavy, the mood might've been uplifting. Jubilant, even.

Back in the sleeping area, the story was different. Many had already retired for the evening, and for the year. These men had deliberately turned in early, so they could close the door on another year sooner, and deal with the coming later. Others sat quietly in their cubes, reading or thinking, bringing in the new year in solitude, sequestered in their own suspended world of prison solitaire. But quiet prevailed.

The starkness between these two groups was a reflection of temperament and reality. You could accurately profile those in the sleeping area, on New Year's Eve at least. They were the lifers and the old timers; seasoned and stoic, unflinching and rehearsed. They were the long-timers, the guys with large stretches of time still looming ahead. For these men, this night meant nothing. It was simply another benchmark to gauge the elevation as they ascended their own mountain of time.

In the recreation room, stereotyping worked and was for once reliable. This raucous room was filled with the laughs and cries of men young and short-term. Those just starting their sentences were often too naive to notice the irony of their celebration, as they cheered in their first new year in prison. This was the first of many, many more to come. For those few who were almost finished with their sentence, they were most right in their joy. For them, this would be the last holiday they'd spend locked-up, away from their families and their lives. But for all, the present reality remained: they were behind bars. They'd been behind bars for yet another year. Another year of time had peeled and fallen from the core of life, never to be recovered.

I sat in my cube and pondered this reality...my reality. I looked back over the prior three New Year's Eves I'd spent in this system of human warehousing. I thought about what they meant, how I'd grown, what I'd learned. I just sat there and I thought. And then it dawned on me, like an incandescent with the flick of a switch: I don't have any New Year's resolutions to make this year.

I understand this may not exactly seem like a game-changing revelation, but for someone who always finds at least a few things about his life he would like to change in the coming year, it was significant. Huge, in fact. I crawled over this realization, trying to glean certainty of my honesty and candor. Did I really have nothing I'd like to resolve to change? That can't be, I thought. So I conducted an abridged personal inventory. This is an exercise I do every so often to check-up on my personal development, you know, see how things are coming along.

Naturally, I began with my health. Most might start with this, since what do we really have if not first our health? I'd now been steadfastly working out and running for almost a year. I hadn't missed one day in my five-on, two-off weekly regimen. I'd further reduced my fat and cholesterol intake. I was eating healthier and my diet was yielding noticeable dividends. I was in the best shape of my life.

Spiritually, I'd arrived at a place unknown to me just three years ago. I'd been a part of a wonderful fellowship of like-minded people for almost two years; a group and its conscience that had helped me grow and mature tremendously. I was finally able to accept my plight and resolve to move forward positively.

Emotionally and mentally, I'd also reached similar levels of contentedness. I sat on that hard slab of steel I had called my bed for three years, and smiled. I recalled a saying my father told me early on as I set out on this corrective journey: *don't count time, make time count.* Terse, but leagues from trite. I made this my unofficial credo for how I wished to live my life behind bars.

The noise of the recreation room would occasionally creep into the sleeping area, breaching the wonderful silence of acceptance. This was usually momentary though. A few might turn to see who the person was, the one in violation of this sacrosanct area, especially on this pregnant evening. Then they'd return to their affairs; their book, their thoughts— not another moment spent on everything this small display of inappropriateness stood for.

One o'clock came and went, and the celebrations persisted. Just as last year grew to a close with such glaring division, so was this year brought in. I glanced around the dimly lit landscape of the dorm's sleeping quarters. Many had now turned in; I thought I ought to do the same. I cleaned my area up quickly. I made a quick stop at the bathroom to wash-up, and found myself again sitting on my bunk, peering out into the possibility of a world beyond the fence.

Things were okay, I thought. I was comfortable and grateful for all I was so fortunate to have in my life: my loving family and wonderful friends, my sanity and my health, my life. A slight smile again found its way to my face. This was finally my year. I was now being given the opportunity to realize my commitments and my dreams, as a free man in the free world. The transition wouldn't be easy, my duty nothing insignificant. But I was confident. I felt at peace and at one with myself and with the situation; I was coming to terms with my life and where it had brought me. I was ready for the next chapter.

I unfurled my sheets and climbed into the crisp envelope of newly washed linens. I closed my eyes... slowly drifting from one domain to another, from one year to the next, keeping the faith strong that things would be all right.

THE KEY TO THE GATES

Don't leave anything out of place in your cube, anything. Do you smoke? No? Good. This guy's a beast, he's an animal. He's more Robocop than correctional officer. Seriously. If you leave anything out, it's his. Or better yet, it's the landfill's. You don't think that he can do that? Just take your property at will? File a grievance then, see how that goes. This is what my new roommate told me. I had just moved, for the fifth time in less than a year. Just when I begin to get comfortable, begin to cultivate some normalcy...*hey you, yeah you, you're moving. Pack your shit.* Every time this seems to happen. I'm beginning to think it's deliberate, you know, a crowd control mechanism...keep everyone guessing, constant flux.

They said he was the dormitory unit's regular 3 to 11 p.m. officer. Wonderful. Five days a week of this guy. How bad could it really be though? I wasn't a troublemaker. I was quiet, to myself, gave no reason to be a target on his radar. The reason for this move was job-related. I had been assigned as a Team Leader on my new floor, which, I would soon find out, sounds much more important than it really is. I was simply another floor porter with an enhanced title. No more pay, absolutely no benefits, and now the added responsibility of several porters beneath me.

By added responsibility, I would come to learn I was simply Gates's whipping boy, the fall guy—the buck stopped with me. When other porters didn't do their jobs, or did them poorly (a daily occurrence), I was the one Gates yelled at. As if I was in some position to tell another inmate what to do. I'm in state greens, just like him; I carry an ID card with an unflattering mug just as he does; I'm not a cop, so I can't tell him to do anything, unless I'm longing for a fight.

Just like they said, at ten to three he showed up. He sauntered onto the unit from the elevator bay. His turquoise playmate cooler in tote didn't go with the whole look he seemed to be going for. He stood about five-ten, maybe slightly shorter with his poor posture. He was obese. I don't mean just overweight, I'm talking government largesse obese...with a nice pension-security paunch. He had on silver framed aviators, usually commanding sunglasses. On him, though, they looked like small reading spectacles, undistinguished amidst the fleshy abundance of his cherubic face. He held a commanding stare down the hallway as he walked slowly to the officer's station, peering back and forth from room to room as he passed. In fairness to the truth, it was actually more of a waddle than a walk. His state blues looked like he'd outgrown them a few years back, but neglected to get new ones. He finally made it to the officer's station, glanced behind and then forward again, and entered.

Well, I might as well go report for duty, I thought. My new work shift didn't start for another half-hour, but I thought being early on my first day wouldn't hurt the first impression. When I got to the edge of the officer's station, I peered inside slowly. I saw Officer Gates unpacking his cooler, cleaning up the mess the last officer had created on the shift prior. I knocked on the door.

"Excuse me," I said.

He snapped his head toward me.

"Who the hell are you? Why are you at my office? Can't you see I just got in?" he said, obviously angered by my presence.

"But I just wanted to—"

"I don't give a shit what you wanted to do. Come back later. Jesus!"

That was it. I had met the feared Officer Gates, and he had met me. Not exactly the good first impression I had been aiming for.

My first of many run-ins with Gates came on my second night on the new unit. I had set up a little office nook in the corner of the recreation room, like I always did on every new dorm I moved to. I had my typewriter, my textbooks, and my coffee. I was studying for a final exam. It was in Business Law, one of the correspondence courses I had been taking through the good old pony express. The exam was the next day at eight in the morning. I had been studying for days, but this was the last-night cram session. I had been at it for hours, and needed a little break. You know, just to get up and walk around, use the bathroom, maybe refill the coffee.

When I returned after no more than five minutes, my typewriter and textbook were missing. Gone, without a trace. I immediately panicked. Had I gotten robbed in just the five minutes I'd been gone? You gotta be kidding me, I thought. I have a test tomorrow morning! A guy I didn't know approached me then, told me Gates took it. He took it all, he said.

"You've gotta be kidding me! What the fuck? I'm studying! I have a final exam in the morning! I couldn't be further from breaking the rules!" I exclaimed!

I was heated, this was ridiculous! I went directly to the officer's station to get back my belongings and continue my studying.

I knocked again, with a little more force this time.

"Oh, it's you again. What do you want now?" Officer Gates said menacingly.

"You've got my typewriter and my textbook, Officer Gates. I am studying for a final exam tomorrow; I need them back."

He just stared ahead at his newspaper, clippings littered all over the desk. He told me how it is against the rules to leave anything out...anything, ever. I pleaded, told him I merely went to the bathroom for five minutes. I'd been doing productive work, studying for a final exam. I was causing absolutely no trouble, but it didn't matter. Nothing gets left out, he kept saying. Nothing. But what about all of the other stuff left out, I thought? What about all of the flotsam of the recreational wreckage strewn about the recreation room? He said he didn't see anything else. He only saw my typewriter and textbook, in their illicit glare as they sat unattended on the table in the corner. Right.

I pleaded, and he ignored. Then he told me to leave, to carry on with my business. Carry on? How am I to carry on without the typewriter and my textbook? I stormed back to my room, with no recourse in sight. This was insane! What is this guy's problem? I told my roommates. They weren't surprised. Weren't surprised? This is ridiculous! I need my stuff! I have a final exam tomorrow! They all told me to calm down and just relax. The more I showed my frustration, the longer it'd be until I got my stuff back. Gates thrived on discontent. Just chill-out, and ask him in a few hours, my roommates told me. Those few hours were valuable hours, but I had no choice. Officer Gates and I had gotten off to a great start.

Over the next few weeks, I really saw what my roommates had been talking about: Gates was a beast! At two-thirty every afternoon, the unit seemed to pulsate with adrenaline as we anticipated his arrival. Rooms were swept, mopped and dusted; laundry was collected and stowed; cubes were straightened; areas were checked, and then checked again. It was like a dormant colony had come alive. It was like clockwork, every day at two-thirty. This wasn't simply a job for Officer Gates, it was a career. This was also a hobby, and most importantly, this was a way of life for him. Gates derived his identity—his sense of self-worth and self-esteem—from his position as correctional officer.

I quickly found working for Gates was no walk in the woods. I was routinely ordered to do tasks outside my responsibilities, those beyond my duties. I caught flack regularly for the subpar performance of the porters under me, again as if I had any authority over them or any ability to tell them what to do.

"Hey, uhh, you think you could spend a little more time cleaning the bathroom? You know, actually clean it?" I might ask.

"Yeah, maybe I could do that, but not before I beat your ass in the bathroom. Take that soap ball and rub it on your chest, Team Leader!"

That's about how it'd go.

Gates continued to pile on the work: clean this, dust that, mop over there, come take out these newspaper clippings from my office...the list went on and on. It got to the point where I needed to find some help, and I sure wasn't going to get it from my fellow porters. Some guys on the floor offered contracts for work details, porter work, washing dishes, et cetera. Almost everyone had a hustle in here, a racket of some sort to earn a little extra cash for food, tobacco or whatever.

I asked one of my roommates if he'd be interested in helping me with some of my porter duties. I told him my offer after running down the jobs to be done: 1 bag of Maxwell House instant coffee every commissary purchase, which was every two weeks. He quickly jumped on it. I had a personal assistant, if you will, for the scant wage of a dollar sixty-four every two weeks, less than half what the State was paying me for the same labor. Fuzzy economics, I know, but inmates are generally averse to unionizing. Everyone is for himself, and himself only, in prison. This is a boon for the employer, as there's always someone willing to do the work for less.

One day I approached Officer Gates's little man cave to tell him I'd finished the daily work, and ask him if he minded if I went to the recreation yard at three-thirty (which was technically still my shift, but I was done with my job). There was a little guy hunched over with two property bags who came in the door from the stairwell, cut right in front of me as he headed for the officer's station too. Another soon-to-be victim of Gates, I thought. This guy better hurry up; they're going to call the recreation movement any minute now.

The short man in front of me peered around the corner into the bubble, like everyone seems to at first, scared of what they may find. He knocked softly on the painted steel door, and then I heard Gates:

"Holy Fuck! You look just like a leprechaun! Jesus Christ! Don't they have a height requirement for this jail? My God!"

I couldn't believe what he had just told this guy, right to his face. I couldn't help but laugh, so I turned away and let it out. Gates was insane, his nerve hilarious. The new guy stood at the doorway, peering at Gates with vacancy, in shock and far from amused. it was probably not the first time this guy had heard this. I mean all he was really missing was a pot of gold and a rainbow.

The vertically challenged guy told Gates he had been moved to this floor, and handed him his ID card. This produced no less funny a reaction.

"Jesus, me picture looks just like ee leprechaun too!"

The little guy began to become visibly annoyed. I couldn't help myself, so I turned again and laughed. He turned around this time and stared right at me. He didn't say anything, but he didn't have to. His eyes said it all. *Fuck you too, asshole!*

Finally, Gates gave him back his ID after another couple of gibes, and directed him toward his new room. I approached and asked Gates if I could go out to the yard. I told him how everything was finished already. He sat there, silently, mulling it over; big decision it was. Finally he looked up, and said yes.

"But don't get used to this, you're technically still on shift until six-thirty," he told me.

Wow! I was a bit surprised, but took the small victory and ran with it. Unfortunately, it was short-lived. I hadn't been outside in that recreation yard for more than ten minutes, when it came roaring over the loudspeaker. The yard froze and everyone stopped what they were doing, waiting to hear who the unlucky dunce was.

"Inmate Weimer, 07A6490, report back to the Dormitory Unit," the speakers broadcast across the crowded yard.

Wonderful, I was that guy today. I commenced the walk of shame back to the unit, not knowing what Gates could possibly find this important to call me back after he just gave me permission to go out. I reported to the officer's station, asked Gates what was wrong.

"I need you to sweep the slop-sink area," he told me.

But I had already done that; I told him I had finished my job.

"Well, do it again," he shot back.

I stared at him as he sat in his chair, exceeding all dimensions and not bothering to look up and make eye contact. You have to be kidding me, I thought but didn't say. I left the officer's station and went about cleaning the slop-sink area—again, twenty minutes after I had done it the first time. This guy's totally lost his beans, I thought. He's the boss from Hell, and he even looks a bit like Cerberus. Unfortunately, it wouldn't be the last time this happened either.

As new people moved onto the floor and others moved off, I fell a few spots on Gate's hierarchy of *people to fuck with*. We got some shady characters that took some of the heat off me. He would pursue them, and they would mess up. They'd be off to solitary confinement, just like that. If they didn't mess-up, Gates would make sure they'd mess up. Either way, if he wanted you gone, he'd find a way to make you vanish, one way or the other. It was as simple as that. Even with these occasional distractions, he didn't relent for long.

I began to notice him call the mail later and later every day, and so did the rest of the inmates on the unit. I would creep up to the officer's station and glance inside, only to see him leaning back on his chair, which was about to give way any second, while reading MY newspaper! *The Wall Street Journal!* Hold up, I'm not paying a yearly subscription so we both can read this… this is no free ride! Furthermore, he was holding up the entire mail distribution just so he could read my paper before he gave it me. Others noticed this quickly, and somehow it became my fault just because it was my paper he was reading, like I could control what he did.

I also began to notice small irregularities. Doodles, to be precise. At first they were subtle: a cloaked mustache on some poor liberal on page twenty of the front section. Maybe Senator Barbara Boxer, at a press conference promoting the health bill, rocking a prominent goatee with her new Vera Wang dress and Jimmy Choos. Or maybe it was Speaker of the House Nancy Pelosi, at a leftist fundraiser in Beverly Hills, sporting her new soul patch, and widow's peak. I ignored it at first. It was actually pretty funny. That was probably the one thing we did have in common, that he leaned right in his political bent.

But it gradually crept its way closer to the front, until one day it was staring right at me: Bam! Obama, front and center—and above the fold—with the horns of the devil and a tail to boot. I had to laugh, as it was kind of funny. But at the same time, it was getting a little carried away. My newspaper was becoming Gates's own personal political Etch-A-Sketch. He had endless liberal fodder to toy with, too, now that Obama had ridden the tidal wave of Bush discontent into the White House and his fellow Dems controlled both houses of Congress. When would this end? Would this end? I had to approach him and say something. If only for the sake of preserving my federal postal rights, this free ride had to end.

I went to the officer's station after the Obama pejorative. I had decided on a strategy before I went: I would use our shared political ideologies to broach a dialogue about the direction of our great country. You know, to sort of divert the attention from what I wasn't doing right, to what Obama wasn't doing right. I had to attempt to broker a peace between us. In short, the idea was brilliant...and it worked! From this crucial juncture in our officer-inmate relationship, Gates seemed less and less inclined to hem-me-up or trap-me-off, as so it goes in here; in other words, he was less likely to write me tickets or send me to the hoosegow within a hoosegow: solitary confinement.

This didn't mean I secured carte blanche, to reign as I saw fit as the favored inmate of Monsieur Gates. No, it was far from that. What did happen was he became less and less of a direct antagonist. He turned into more of a resident ball-buster. Less beast, more jester. Others would only wish they could attain this coveted treatment. I caught a lot of flack for it from the other inmates as a result, but I had to navigate this sea on my own, and survive this gauntlet alone.

Things gradually became less stressful when Gates was on, which seemed like every day. Did this guy ever take vacation days? He honestly would sometimes work six, seven days in a row. I think he really enjoyed working so much he'd volunteer to come in and cover for the sick call-ins on his days off; earn that time-and-a-half and get some recreation in the process. He'd write a few tickets, maybe some cube-standard violations, maybe even send someone to solitary confinement with his characteristic caprice, if he was in a really good mood.

The good thing is, I was no longer on the serious, usual suspect dossier. And yes, officer Gates kept a dossier. In fact it was a very detailed, comprehensive log. We called it The Warning Log. He sometimes let this slip after catching someone in flagrante delicto, after having decided to show mercy and refrain from writing them a ticket or sending them to solitary confinement. If he decided to cut you a break, for whatever arbitrary reason, he'd simply record the incident, date and details in the dossier. You better believe this would be your one and only warning.

This thing went back years. I mean four, maybe five years. He had files and dirt on nearly everyone under his purview. It was beyond creepy. Sometimes you wouldn't even know you'd been logged in the Warning Log. Gates would do this often, in a very clandestine manner. We called this a secret indictment, and when handed-up, it was usually devastating. It was disturbingly detailed, with little room for the accused to defend himself against the allegations. Sometimes he'd even slug you without you knowing, deliver the secret indictment directly up to the hearing Lieutenant without notifying you. You'd be lying on your bunk, reading or doing something else, and out of nowhere be called to report to a Lieutenant's Hearing to answer the charges lodged against you. Charges? Lodged against me? What the hell are you talking about? This happened all too often, and one day I learned through the covert reconnaissance of a fellow inmate that I was the latest defendant to be named in one.

For the past few days, I had been going out to the yard after I finished my porter duties. Maybe for a light jog or just to walk around and get off the unit. Well, I had gotten out of the habit of asking Officer Gates for permission. I kind of would just slip off the unit furtively, hoping to return undetected among the throngs of inmates on the recreation movement. I knew this was risky, and looking back in retrospect, don't know how I'd mustered the gall. This one particular day I had returned, without distinction among the multitude. There was nothing out of the ordinary whatsoever.

Then after chow, a couple hours after the yard, a neighbor named Jimmy came running into my room. Jimmy was quite the character. He was generally disliked by almost everyone on the dorm, for one reason or another. He had napalmed every last bridge in here, just as he had with his family and friends on the street. He was a panhandler of the most degenerate degree. He would immediately liquidate any package he'd be fortunate to receive, after basically extorting it from his codependent mother or girlfriend. He'd have everything sold on the local dormitory market so he could procure the two things that drove him and his behavior, his jet fuel: coffee and cigarettes. Then he'd drink and smoke this in a matter of days, relegated to begging again to support his habits until he could manipulate another package out of his loved ones. He was definitely a hardcore drug addict in the streets. It looked to me like it was probably crack-cocaine. It was almost tragic, save for the complete want of any attempt at recovery... sobriety...sanity.

Jimmy came rushing in without knocking, as per usual. He was practically screaming my name. I had been relaxing on my bunk I remember, reading some correspondence I had just received. I had heard him approaching from down the hall as he called me by my last name, in his thick and ever-annoying Brooklyn dialect. The "er" at the end of my last name somehow morphed into an "a." It had gone from Weimer to Weima. He told me how he'd just been spying on Officer Gates, and that he saw my name on the top of a ticket. A secret indictment he said he saw, for me! Fuck, I thought. He must have found out about the yard. How could I have honestly thought he wouldn't?

"Are you sure it's my name, Jimmy?" I asked him.

"Positive," he said. "It says Weima on top."

"You mean Weimer, Jimmy?" I said back.

"Yeah, what I said, Weima."

"Whatever, Jimmy," I said in frustration.

I asked him nervously what the charges were. He said he couldn't make them out from his perch, but there were multiple charges, he said. Great, I thought, a multi-count secret indictment from Officer Gates. I started to panic a bit. I had an approaching parole board hearing in a couple of months. This would definitely be a damning strike on my record. I had to do something. I had to talk to him, explain my reasoning, as flawed as it was. To think he wouldn't find out, how could I have been so stupid? Now I know what the other inmates mean, when they jokingly say they'd never commit a crime with me. I do make a pretty lousy criminal.

Jimmy tried to calm me down. He actually persuaded me to hold-off from approaching the *Gatestapo* for now. He said he could steal the ticket from Gates, after he had written it and left it in the box for the sergeant to sign and take away on his evening rounds.

"Steal the ticket? Are you crazy? What is wrong with you, Jimmy?" I told him.

As if he won't notice something's up when I never get called down to the hearing; when I don't return all downtrodden to the unit, with the hearing disposition in hand, multiple sanctions in place. This is why he writes tickets and indictments as often as he does. Gates lives for this moment. This is his positive reinforcement, confirming he's an integral component of the correctional machine.

"This is a horrible idea, Jimmy. No. Out of the question. You are not stealing the ticket, no matter what. Okay?" I tell him angrily.

"Alright, fine," Jimmy told me.

Not a half-hour later, Jimmy comes bursting in my room, ticket in hand.

"I got it! I got it, Weima! Look! Look!"

"Holy shit Jimmy! You gotta be kidding me, what the hell did I tell you? Are you deaf? Did you not hear anything I said?"

I became pretty angry at this point, at Jimmy's open defiance, and at my worsening situation. I really started to panic. Jimmy kept interjecting as I thought out loud the ramifications of his act. This was clearly not the first time he'd stolen a ticket from Gates as it awaited a sergeant's signature.

"Listen, listen, he'll never know," he kept saying, with nothing else in support of his words, as if that was trustworthy counsel.

"Thanks for the reassurance Jimmy, it's very comforting. Asshole," I said to him.

After we argued and I became more angry, I told Jimmy to get out of my room, told him to leave and let me be. He finally acquiesced, after I basically had to threaten him. I sat on my bed, worried and wondering. How am I to get out of this developing pickle? Look what this has progressed into. This is definitely solitary confinement territory now. What about my parole? Fuck!

Then, all of a sudden, who appears at the threshold to my room? It's Officer Gates, with Jimmy in close tow. I stood up, worried sick about what was about to happen. Then Gates slowly began to smile. He told me it was all a big joke, and it was all on me.

"Gotcha!" Gates said with a huge smile and cackle. Jimmy started laughing uncontrollably behind him, keeling over in a fit of glee. I couldn't believe it, I had been had, and bad!

This is what our relationship evolved into, which was much better than the alternative. I could put up with this, after a little getting used to. Hell, it sure beat solitary confinement. I smiled, and laughed, and entertained his dumb, often racist jokes. This was out of a need to survive; my fate was uniquely in his hands, under his control for the time being. One false move, one slip of resentment, and the scales could be shifted on a dime. I'd become a target again, placed on the most popular list in The Warning Log, maybe even be headed for a stretch in solitary confinement. I felt like I was walking on eggshells much of the time with his mercurial personality.

I gradually learned more about Gates as time went on. I learned more about his character, his habits, his pathologies. This guy had serious issues, beyond the obvious social deviancy of his personality. One day I had to get his John Hancock on a disbursement form to release funds from my commissary account. I approached the officer's station with my usual reservation. I peered in before knocking, as I always did.

Only this time it was different. I was frozen by what I saw. The office was in shambles, like it'd just been hit by some random western New York microburst. There were newspaper clippings, by the hundreds, strewn all about the small room; files were scattered about; stacks of articles arranged by subject with heading; folders opened all over the floor.

Gates was sitting on his diminutive stool, hunched over the antiquated steel desk that screamed of needless bureaucracy. With scissors in hand, he was dissecting the latest victim: today's Buffalo News newspaper. The scene was so eerie I almost gasped, but I managed to catch myself. It looked like something straight out of *Silence of the Lambs.* At any moment, it wouldn't have surprised me if Gates opened the trapdoor to his secret dungeon, and screamed down to some hapless inmate at the bottom..."It puts the lotion on its skin...it does what it's told!"

I quickly decided I needed to get the hell out of there, and the disbursement form was swiftly forgotten. After that incident I kept my distance. Not obviously, but I was cautious. I mean this guy might have bodies buried in his backyard for all I know. His state blue uniform could just be a front for his sociopathic proclivities.

Things continued the way they'd been going. They were relatively even-keeled, until one particular night. I'd been having difficulty sleeping, staying asleep for longer than a couple of hours. I kept tossing, getting up to use the bathroom. Well, I got up once and turned to face the piercing beam of a Maglite pointed directly into my eyes from the doorway. It was Gates.

"What the fuck?" I said in astonishment.

He quickly turned and scurried away, saying nothing. Alright, this is getting weird, I thought. There is something seriously wrong with this guy. Stay calm, I thought. Any day you'll be shipped out of here, on your long awaited transfer. Sure enough, not a week after this latest incident, I got a call to the officer's station. Gates was on. I answered him at the doorway to his grotto.

"You're on the transfer draft. Pack your shit and report to draft process," he told me without looking up.

I was immediately relieved.

"You know where you're going, right?" he asked, as he looked up at me with more interest.

I told him I did. I was going to a minimum-security facility closer to home.

"That's what you think. Think again. Hahahahaha. I called down and found out where you're headed. You're going to Attica, the most notorious maximum-security prison in the state," he said as he began to laugh.

It was a controlled chortle at first, but quickly grew into a deep, maleficent cackle. It honestly scared me. He scared me. The news scared me. I tried to ask him details, but he waved me off as he whaled in merriment. This guy is sick. I turned and left to gather my belongings and report to draft process.

I left the next morning, and not for Attica. Gates couldn't let me go without one last ribbing; he simply had to get in one more feint. It was only natural. Officer Gates certainly wasn't the most peculiar person I'd met along this journey, but he took the blue ribbon for most bizarre. I boarded the correctional transfer bus, headed for the next stop on my corrective passage. I was shackled, but free. I was free from Gates—from his emotional and psychological tyranny—knowing this leg was over, but not knowing what was still to come.

THE POWER OF FREEDOM

He'd dreamt of faraway lands and seas unknown. He was often the skipper of a sloop, with a crew of one, roaming an open expanse of waters far and foreign. Sometimes he'd hug the comforting shores of the French Riviera, or venture into the uncertain depths of the Adriatic off the Peninsula's eastern cliffs. Maybe he'd simply sail without purpose, without direction, until his heart was content. Sometimes this was all it took, all he needed to keep him moving forward. The absolute power of freedom eludes description.

Those dreams and these visions had been his guide for almost three decades. He'd never been to the places he imagined, but had read all about them. He'd read of them numerous times. He had promised himself he'd go whenever he got out. When that glorious day would arrive he still knew not, but he promised…and he persevered. One step at a time, one day at a time, until that day came; a day when no day that followed would ever be the same. This was the day of his release.

He slept maybe an hour, two at most, he thought. How could he have slept, knowing today was the day: the first day of the rest of his life. He rose before the sun, beat it by almost two hours. He had two cups of coffee in him before it even peeked over the distant horizon. Today was the same as any other, and yet couldn't be more unique.

The dorm came to life as it usually did. The wave of fluorescents firing up pulled the collective consciousness along with it—reluctantly, but with it. The morose mugs of fifty-nine fellow inmates were instantly put on display. This exhibit was a reminder, fully lit for all to take in and promptly end any wayward reality. All fifty-nine. But there were sixty men in the dorm. Sixty. The old man was the lone outlier. He was the very occasional straggler who, for reasons only he knew, was able to escape the strong force of the correctional bell curve. Today he was that outlier, and today he'd be the single datum to forever fall from the chart and the count. He'd be promptly replaced by some new number, some new soul just beginning his long journey in purgatory, where Virgil as guide had long since departed.

He sat in his cube, waiting for that call he'd been anticipating for twenty-eight years. The usual suspects came and went, and the usual nothings were exchanged, and exchanged again. But the old man sat, motionless in his now emptied cube...waiting, and then it came. The telephone ring sounded more like a Siren's cry from Grecian lore than a staid prison phone, piercing the air, and finally answering the patient anticipation of one near-broken soul. He knew the call was for him before its announcement was broadcast over the dormitory's loudspeaker. He stood up with a certain deliberateness foreign even to him. Heads turned as he approached the officer's desk to confirm the order.

It happened just as he'd imagined it would. He turned away from the officer's desk, and a smile pushed its way through the heavy folds of a worn face. Others now began to take notice. This smile was out of place, something was askew; but only in their twisted reception. The old man hadn't told anyone when he was going home. No one. For many reasons, but none worthy of note. Whispers turned to chatter, and people began to move...talk and question. Was the old man going home? No, he couldn't be. They'd never let him out for what he did to that poor man, in that fit of drunken rage. No, probably just a transfer, they mused.

He quickly gathered what little he had. It fit nicely into two old nylon corn sacks. He carefully tied them together, and hoisted them over his sunken shoulders. He took one last glance at his cube...the dorm...the faces among which he'd existed for those twenty-eight empty years. Then he turned and headed for the door. Only then did the others realize where he was going, and what was happening. The faces then grew tight and the eyes narrow. As much as anyone said they loved to see the next man go home, everyone knew this was a lie. No one enjoyed watching another get to leave the confines of a life devoid of liberty. No one found joy in facing the reality of his own continuing imprisonment. They grew envious and sad, jealous and angry, every time.

After a few curt exchanges, he emerged from the dorm. He came into this world alone, and was now leaving alone. He'd made acquaintances, sure, maybe even a few he'd consider friends over his lengthy bid. But he still had done this alone, had lived and survived this alone, and was now leaving this dark underworld alone.

The crisp morning air was dry and refreshing. The old man stood for a moment at the door. He took a few deep breaths, readjusted the satchels on his shoulders, and then he was off. He walked confidently and with purpose, for the first time in a very, very long time, because now the old man had a purpose and an end. It was no longer the hopelessness of not knowing when he'd arrive. It was certain and solid as concrete. He passed a few inmates on the walkway, as he made for the administration building, where the portal to a life worth living existed.

When he reached the gate, he paused. He turned around, and took in the abyss he'd finally found egress from. Finally, after all these years. The gate latch buzzed, as he turned to open the heavy door and proceed. He walked through to the next gate, and waited again. He knew not to look back now. The second gate sounded as he again opened and proceeded. The heavy metal gate slammed shut behind him, with a certain finality ordinarily unsettling. But today it wasn't. Right now it was comforting. He was finally on the other side. From here forward, he'd be the one locking the door—from the inside.

He stepped up and into the administration building, a building he'd never been in before, and one he'd never see again. He approached another set of gates. He waded through this second man-trap, and emerged on the outer bank of a world he'd called home for almost half his life. He was swiftly beckoned to the desk, the last hurdle to a world uninhibited. The old man was told to sign here, here and here... which he did after a cursory glance at the release paper heading. He knew this was merely a formality; it was just one last order he'd be obliged to obey. Then he was told good luck by an expressionless drone clad in state blue, told the bus would be by at the top of the hour.

He again shouldered his two bags of property, and headed for the bench on the other side of the building. A bench he'd only seen through the distortion of four chain-link fences topped with a steady ribbon of piercing razor wire. A bench that would be the first bench he sat on as a free man. He stood for a moment at the threshold to life. He gazed around at the cars that looked like space ships, and then he turned around, one last time. To peer back into the cave of his past twenty-eight years. To now forever detach himself and his identity from a world marked only by the absence of both.